JOAN JOHNSTON
THE TEMPORARY GROOM

SILHOUETTE *Desire*

Published by Silhouette Books

America's Publisher of Contemporary Romance

This book is dedicated to
Anne,
who learned to enjoy books at the age of 37 when she began reading romance novels, and who has since decided to return to school and continue her education.

 SILHOUETTE BOOKS

ISBN 0-373-76004-3

THE TEMPORARY GROOM

Copyright © 1996 by Joan Mertens Johnston

Printed in U.S.A.

JOAN JOHNSTON

started reading romances to escape the stress of being an attorney with a major national law firm. She soon discovered that writing romances was a lot more fun than writing legal bond indentures. Since then, she has published a number of historical and contemporary category romances. In addition to being an author, Joan is the mother of two children. In her spare time, she enjoys sailing, horseback riding and camping.

Hawk's Way Family Tree

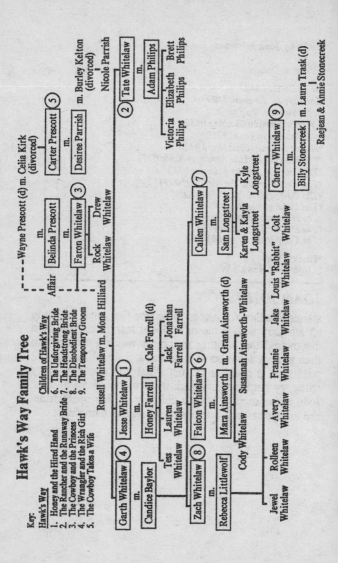

Key:

Hawk's Way
1. Honey and the Hired Hand
2. The Rancher and the Runaway Bride
3. The Cowboy and the Princess
4. The Wrangler and the Rich Girl
5. The Cowboy Takes a Wife

Children of Hawk's Way
6. The Unforgiving Bride
7. The Headstrong Bride
8. The Disobedient Bride
9. The Temporary Groom

Russell Whitelaw m. Mona Hilliard

- - - Wayne Prescott (d) m. Celia Kirk (divorced)

⑤ Carter Prescott m. Belinda Prescott — Affair

⑤ m. Desiree Parrish

② Tate Whitelaw m. Burley Kelton (divorced) — Nicole Parrish

③ Faron Whitelaw — Rock Whitelaw, Drew Whitelaw

Adam Philips m. Elizabeth Philips — Victoria Philips, Brett Philips

① Jesse Whitelaw m. Honey Farrell m. Cale Farrell (d) — Jack Farrell, Jonathan Farrell

Tess Whitelaw, Lauren Whitelaw

④ Garth Whitelaw m. Candice Baylor

⑥ Falcon Whitelaw m. Mara Ainsworth m. Grant Ainsworth (d) — Susannah Ainsworth-Whitelaw, Cody Whitelaw

⑦ Callen Whitelaw m. Sam Longstreet — Karen & Kayla Longstreet, Kyle Longstreet

⑧ Zach Whitelaw m. Rebecca Littlewolf

Jewel Whitelaw, Rolleen Whitelaw, Avery Whitelaw, Frannie Whitelaw, Jake Whitelaw, Louis "Rabbit" Whitelaw, Colt Whitelaw

⑨ Cherry Whitelaw m. Billy Stonecreek m. Laura Trask (d) — Raejean & Annie Stonecreek

One

—

Cherry Whitelaw was in trouble. Again. She simply couldn't live up to the high expectations of her adoptive parents, Zach and Rebecca Whitelaw. She had been a Whitelaw for three years, ever since her fifteenth birthday, and it was getting harder and harder to face the looks of disappointment on her parents' faces each time they learned of her latest escapade.

This time it was really serious. This was about the worst thing that could happen to a high school girl. Well, the second worst. At least she wasn't pregnant.

Cherry had been caught spiking the punch at the senior prom this evening by the principal, Mr. Cornwell, and expelled on the spot. The worst of it was, she wasn't even guilty! Not that anyone was going to believe her. Because most of the time she was.

Her best friend, Tessa Ramos, had brought the pint bottle of whiskey to the dance. Cherry had been trying to talk Tessa out of spiking the punch—had just taken the bottle from Tessa's hand—when Mr. Cornwell caught her with it.

He had snatched it away with a look of dismay and said, "I'm ashamed of you, young lady. It's bad enough when your behavior disrupts class. An irresponsible act like this has farther-reaching ramifications."

"But, Mr. Cornwell, I was only—"

"You're obviously incorrigible, Ms. Whitelaw."

Cherry hated being called that. *Incorrigible.* Being *incorrigible* meant no one wanted her because she was too much trouble. Except Zach and Rebecca had. They had loved her no matter what she did. They would believe in her this time, too. But that didn't change the fact she had let them down. Again.

"You're expelled," Mr. Cornwell had said, his rotund face nearly as red as Cherry's hair, but not quite, because nothing could ever be quite that red. "You will leave this dance at once. I'll be in touch with your parents tomorrow."

No amount of argument about her innocence had done any good, because she had been unwilling to name her best friend as the real culprit. She might be a troublemaker, but she was no rat.

Mr. Cornwell's pronouncement had been final. She was out. She wasn't going to graduate with the rest of her class. She would have to come back for summer school.

Rebecca was going to cry when she found out. And Zach was going to get that grim-lipped look that meant he was really upset.

Cherry felt a little like crying herself. She had no idea why she was so often driven to wild behavior. She only knew she couldn't seem to stop. And it wasn't going to do any good to protest her innocence this time. She had been guilty too often in the past.

"Hey, Cherry! You gonna sit there mopin' all night, or what?"

Cherry glanced at her prom date, Ray Estes. He lay sprawled on the grass beside her at the stock pond on the farthest edge of Hawk's Pride, her father's ranch, where she had retreated in defeat. Her full-length, pale green chiffon prom dress, which had made her feel like a fairy princess earlier in the evening, was stained with dirt and grass.

Ray's tuxedo was missing the jacket, bow tie, and cummerbund, and his shirt was unbuttoned halfway to his waist. He was guzzling the fourth can of a six-pack of beer he had been slowly but surely consuming since they had arrived at the pond an hour ago.

Cherry sat beside him holding the fifth can, but it was still nearly full. Somehow she didn't feel much like getting drunk. She had to face her parents sometime tonight, and that would only be adding insult to injury.

"C'mon, Cherry, give us a li'l kiss," Ray said, dragging himself upright with difficulty and leaning toward her.

She braced a palm in the smooth center of his chest to keep him from falling onto her. "You're drunk, Ray."

Ray grinned. "Shhure am. How 'bout that kiss, Cher-ry?"

"No, Ray."

"Awww, why not?"

"I got thrown out of school tonight, Ray. I don't feel like kissing anybody."

"Not even me?" Ray said.

Cherry laughed at the woeful, hangdog look on his face and shook her head. "Not even you." Ray was good fun most of the time. He drank a little too much, and he drove a little too fast, and his grades hadn't been too good. But she hadn't been in a position to be too picky.

She had dreamed sometimes of what it might be like to be one of the "good girls" and have "nice boys" calling her up to ask for dates. It hadn't happened. She was the kind of trouble nice boys stayed away from.

"C'mon, Cher-ry," Ray said. "Gimme li'l kiss."

He teetered forward, and the sheer weight of him forced her backward so she was lying flat on the ground. Cherry was five-eleven in her stocking feet and could run fast enough to make the girls' track team—if she hadn't always been in too much trouble to qualify. But Ray was four inches taller and forty pounds heavier. She turned her head away to avoid his slobbery, seeking lips, which landed on her cheeks and chin.

"I said no, Ray. Get off!" She shoved uselessly at his heavy body, a sense of panic growing inside her.

"Awww, Cher-ry," he slurred drunkenly. "You know you want it." His hand closed around her breast.

"Ray! No!" she cried. She grabbed his wrist and yanked it away and heard the chiffon rip as his grasping fingers held fast to the cloth. "Ray, please!" she pleaded.

Then she felt his hand on her bare flesh. "No, Ray. No!"

"Gonna have you, Cher-ry," Ray muttered. "Always wanted to. Know you want it, too."

Cherry suddenly realized she might be in even worse trouble than she'd thought.

Billy Stonecreek was in trouble. Again. His former mother-in-law, Penelope Trask, was furious because he had gotten into a little fight in a bar in town and spent the night in jail—for the third time in a year.

He had a live-in housekeeper to stay with his daughters, so they were never alone. He figured he'd been a pretty damned good single parent to his six-year-old twins, Raejean and Annie, ever since their mother's death a year ago. But you'd never know it to hear Penelope talk.

Hell, a young man of twenty-five who worked hard on his ranch from dawn to dusk all week deserved to sow a few wild oats at week's end. His ears rang with the memory of their confrontation in his living room earlier that evening.

"You're a drunken half-breed," Penelope snapped, "not fit to raise my grandchildren. And if I have anything to say about it, you won't have them for much longer!"

Billy felt a burning rage that Penelope should say such a thing while Raejean and Annie were standing right there listening. Especially since he hadn't been the least bit drunk. He'd been looking for a fight, all right, and he'd found it in a bar, but that was all.

There was no hope his daughters hadn't heard Penelope. Their Nintendo game continued on the living room TV, but both girls were staring wide-eyed at him. "Raejean. Annie. Go upstairs while I talk to Nana."

"But, Daddy—" Raejean began. She was the twin who took control of every situation.

"Not a word," he said in a firm voice. "Go."

Annie's dark brown eyes welled with tears. She was the twin with the soft heart.

He wanted to pick them both up and hug them, but he forced himself to point an authoritative finger toward the doorway. "Upstairs and get your baths and get ready for bed. Mrs. Motherwell will be up to help in a minute." He had hired the elderly woman on the spot when he heard her name. She had proven equal to it.

Raejean shot him a reproachful look, took Annie's hand, and stomped out of the room with Annie trailing behind her.

Once they were gone, Billy turned his attention back to his nemesis. "What is it this time, Penelope?"

"This time! What is it every time? You drove my Laura to kill herself, and now you're neglecting my grandchildren. I've had it. I went to see a lawyer today. I've filed for custody of my granddaughters."

A chill of foreboding crawled down Billy's spine. "You've done what?"

"You heard me. I want custody of Raejean and Annie."

"Those are my children you're talking about."

"They'll have a better life with me than they will with a half-breed like you."

"Being part Comanche isn't a crime, Penelope. Lots of people in America are part something. Hell, you're probably part Irish or English or French yourself."

"Your kind has a reputation for not being able to hold their liquor. Obviously, it's a problem for you, too. I don't intend to let my grandchildren suffer for it."

A flush rose on Billy's high, sharp cheekbones. He refused to defend himself. It was none of Penelope's business whether he drank or not. But he didn't. He went looking for a fight when the pain built up inside, and he needed a release for it. But he chose men able to defend themselves, he fought clean, and he willingly paid the damages afterward.

He hated the idea of kowtowing to Penelope, but he didn't want a court battle with her, either. She and her husband, Harvey Trask, were wealthy; he was not. In fact, the Trasks had given this ranch—an edge carved from the larger Trask ranching empire—as a wedding present to their daughter, Laura, thereby ensuring that the newlyweds would stay close to home.

He had resented their generosity at first, but he had grown to love the land, and now he was no more willing to give up the Stonecreek Ranch than he was to relinquish his children.

But his behavior over the past year couldn't stand much scrutiny. He supposed the reason he had started those few barroom brawls wouldn't matter to a judge. And he could never have revealed to anyone the personal pain that had led to such behavior. So he had no excuses to offer Penelope—or a family court judge, either.

"Look, Penelope, I'm sorry. What if I promise—"

"Don't waste your breath. I never wanted my daughter to marry a man like you in the first place. My granddaughters deserve to be raised in a wholesome household where they won't be exposed to your kind."

"What kind is that?" Billy asked pointedly.

"The kind that doesn't have any self-respect, and therefore can't pass it on to their children."

Billy felt his stomach roll. It was a toss-up whether he felt more humiliated or furious at her accusation. "I have plenty of self-respect."

"Could have fooled me!" Penelope retorted.

"I'm not letting you take my kids away from me."

"You can't stop me." She didn't argue with him further, simply headed for the front door—she never used the back, as most people in this part of Texas did. "I'll see you in court, Billy."

Then she was gone.

Billy stood in the middle of the toy-strewn living room, furnished with the formal satin-covered couches and chairs Laura had chosen, feeling helpless. Moments later he was headed for the back door. He paused long enough to yell up the stairs, "I'm going out, Mrs. Motherwell. Good night, Raejean. Good night, Annie."

"Good night, Daddy!" the two of them yelled back from the bathtub in unison.

Mrs. Motherwell appeared at the top of the stairs. "Don't forget this is my last week, Mr. Stonecreek. You'll need to find someone else starting Monday morning."

"I know, Mrs. Motherwell," Billy said with a sigh. He had Penelope to thank for that, too. She had filled Mrs. Motherwell's head with stories about him being a dangerous savage. His granite-hewn features, his untrimmed black hair, his broad shoulders and immense height, and a pair of dark, brooding eyes did nothing to dispel the image. But he couldn't help how he looked. "Don't worry, Mrs. Motherwell. I'll find someone to replace you."

He was the one who was worried. How was he going to find someone as capable as Mrs. Motherwell in a week? It had taken him a month to find her.

He let the kitchen screen door slam and gunned the engine in his black pickup as he drove away. But he couldn't escape his frenetic thoughts.

I'll be damned if I let Penelope take my kids away from me. Who does she think she is? How dare she threaten to steal my children!

He knew his girls needed a mother. Sometimes he missed Laura so much it made his gut ache. But no other woman could ever take her place. He had hired a series of good housekeeper/nannies one after another—it was hard to get help to stay at his isolated ranch—and he and his girls had managed fine.

Or they would, if Penelope and Harvey Trask would leave them alone.

Unfortunately, Penelope blamed him for Laura's death. She had been killed instantly in a car accident that had looked a whole lot like a suicide. Billy had tried telling Penelope that Laura hadn't killed herself, but his mother-in-law hadn't believed him. Penelope Trask had said she would see that he was punished for making Laura so miserable she had taken her own life. Now she was threatening to take his children from him.

He couldn't bear to lose Raejean and Annie. They were the light of his life and all he had left of Laura. God, how he had loved her!

Billy pounded his fist on the steering wheel of his pickup. How could he have been so stupid as to give Penelope the ammunition she needed to shoot him down in court?

It was too late to do anything about his wild reputation. But he could change his behavior. He could stop brawling in bars. If only there were some way he could show the judge he had turned over a new leaf....

Billy didn't drive in any particular direction, yet he eventually found himself at the stock pond he shared with Zach Whitelaw's ranch. The light from the rising moon and stars made a silvery reflection on the center of the pond and revealed the shadows of several pin oaks that surrounded it. He had always found the sounds of the bullfrogs and the crickets and the lapping water soothing to his inner turmoil. He had gone there often to think in the year since Laura had died.

His truck headlights revealed someone else had discovered his sanctuary. He smiled wistfully when he realized a couple was lying together on the grass. He felt a stab of envy. He and Laura had spent their share of stolen moments on the banks of this stock pond when the land had belonged to her father.

He almost turned the truck around, because he wanted to be alone, but there was something about the movements of the couple on the ground that struck him as odd. It took him a moment to realize they weren't struggling in the throes of passion. The woman was trying to fight the man off!

He hit the brakes, shoved open his truck door, and headed for them on the run. He hadn't quite reached the girl when he heard her scream of outrage.

He grabbed hold of the boy by his shoulders and yanked him upright. The tall, heavyset kid came around swinging.

That was a mistake.

Billy ducked and came up underneath with a hard fist to the belly that dropped the kid to his knees. A second later the boy toppled face-forward with a groan.

Billy made a sound of disgust that the kid hadn't put up more of a fight and hurried to help the girl. She had curled in on herself, her body rigid with tension. When he put a hand on her shoulder, she tried scrambling away.

"He's not going to hurt you anymore," he said in the calm, quiet voice he used when he was gentling horses. He turned her over so she could see she was safe from the boy, that he was there to help. Her torn bodice exposed half of a small, well-formed breast. He made himself look away, but his body tightened responsively. Her whole body began to tremble.

"Shh. It's all right. I'm here now."

She looked up at him with eyes full of pain.

"Are you hurt?" he asked, his hands doing a quick once-over for some sign of injury.

She slapped at him ineffectually with one hand while holding the torn chiffon against her nakedness with the other. "No. I'm fine. Just...just..."

Her eyes—he couldn't tell what color they were in the dark—filled with tears and, despite her desperate attempts to blink the moisture away, one sparkling teardrop spilled onto her cheek. It was then he realized the pain he had seen wasn't physical, but came from inside.

He understood that kind of pain all too well.

"Hey," he said gently. "It's going to be all right."

"Easy for you to say," she snapped, rubbing at the tears and swiping them across her cheeks. "I—"

A car engine revved, and they both looked toward the sound in time to see a pair of headlights come on.

"Wait!" the girl cried, surging to her feet.

The dress slipped, and Billy got an unwelcome look at a single, luscious breast. He swore under his breath as his body hardened.

The girl obviously wasn't used to long dresses, because the length of it caught under her knees and trapped her on the ground. By the time she made it to her feet, the car she had come in, and the boy she had come with, were gone.

He took one look at her face in the moonlight and saw a kind of desolation he hadn't often seen before.

Except perhaps in his own face in the mirror.

It made his throat ache. It might have brought him to tears, if he had been the kind of man who could cry. He wasn't. He thought maybe his Comanche heritage had something to do with it. Or maybe it was simply a lack of feeling in him. He didn't know. He didn't want to know.

As he watched, the girl sank to the ground and dropped her face into her hands. Her shoulders rocked with soundless, shuddering sobs.

He settled beside her, not speaking, not touching, merely a comforting presence, there if she needed him. Occasionally he heard a sniffling sound, but otherwise he was aware of the silence. And finally, the sounds he had come to hear. The bullfrogs. The crickets. The water lapping in the pond.

He didn't know how long he had been sitting beside her when she finally spoke.

"Thank you," she said.

Her voice was husky from crying, and rasped over him, raising the hairs on his neck. He looked at her again and saw liquid, shining eyes in a pretty face. He couldn't keep his gaze from dropping to the flesh revealed by her tightened grip on the torn fabric. Hell, he was a man, not a saint.

"Are you all right?" he asked.

She shook her head, gave a halfhearted laugh, and said, "Sure." The sarcasm in her voice made it plain she was anything but.

"Can I help?"

"I'd need a miracle to get me out of the mess I'm in." She shrugged, a surprisingly sad gesture. "I can't seem to stay out of trouble."

He smiled sympathetically. *I have the same problem.* He thought the words, but he didn't say them. He didn't want to frighten her. "Things happen," he said instead.

She reached out hesitantly to touch a recent cut above his eye. "Did Ray do this?"

He edged back from her touch. It felt too good. "No. That's from—" *Another fight.* He didn't finish that thought aloud, either. "Something else."

He had gotten a whiff of her perfume. Something light and flowery. Something definitely female. It reminded him he hadn't been with a woman since

Laura's death. And that he found the young woman sitting beside him infinitely desirable.

He tamped down his raging hormones. She needed his help. She didn't need another male lusting after her.

She reached for an open can of beer sitting in the grass nearby and lifted it to her lips.

Before it got there, he took it from her. "Aren't you a little young for this?"

"What difference does it make now? My life is ruined."

He smiled indulgently. "Just because your boyfriend—"

"Ray's not my boyfriend. And he's the least of my problems."

He raised a questioning brow. "Oh?"

He watched her grasp her full lower lip in her teeth—and wished he were doing it himself. He forced his gaze upward to meet with hers.

"I'm a disappointment to my parents," she said in a whispery, haunted voice.

How could such a beautiful—he had been looking at her long enough to realize she was more than pretty—young woman be a disappointment to anybody? "Who are your parents?"

"I'm Cherry Whitelaw."

She said it defiantly, defensively. And he knew why. She had been the talk of the neighborhood—the "juvenile delinquent" the Whitelaws had taken into their home four years ago, the most recently adopted child of their eight adopted children.

"If you're trying to scare me off, it won't work." He grinned and said, "I'm Billy Stonecreek."

The smile grew slowly on her face. He saw the moment when she relaxed and held out her hand. "It's nice to meet you, Mr. Stonecreek. I used to see you in church with your—" She cut herself off.

"It's all right to mention my wife," he said. But he knew why she had hesitated. Penelope's tongue had been wagging, telling anyone who would listen how he had caused Laura to kill herself. Cherry's lowered eyes made it obvious she had heard the stories. He didn't know why he felt the urge to defend himself to her when he hadn't to anyone else.

"I had nothing to do with Laura's death. It was simply a tragic accident." Then, before he could stop himself, "I miss her."

Cherry laid a hand on his forearm, and he felt the muscles tense beneath her soothing touch. She waited for him to look at her before she spoke. "I'm sorry about your wife, Mr. Stonecreek. It must be awful to lose someone you love."

"Call me Billy," he said, unsure how to handle her sympathy.

"Then you have to call me Cherry," she said with the beginnings of a smile. She held out her hand. "Deal?"

"Deal." He took her hand and held it a moment too long. Long enough to realize he didn't want to let go. He forced himself to sit back. He raised the beer can he had taken from her to his lips, but she took it from him before he could tip it up.

"I don't think this will solve your problems, either," she said with a cheeky grin.

He laughed. "You're right."

They smiled at each other.

Until Billy realized he wanted to kiss her about as bad as he had ever wanted anything in his life. His smile faded. He saw the growing recognition in her eyes and turned away. He was there to rescue the girl, not to ravish her.

He picked a stem of sweet grass and twirled it between his fingertips. "Would you like to talk about what you've done that's going to disappoint your parents?"

She shrugged. "Hell. Why not?"

The profanity surprised him. Until he remembered she hadn't been a Whitelaw for very long. "I'm listening."

Her eyes remained focused on her tightly laced fingers. "I got expelled from high school tonight."

He let out a breath he hadn't realized he'd been holding. "That's pretty bad, all right. What did you do?"

"Nothing! Not that I'm innocent all that often, but this time I was. Just because I had a whiskey bottle in my hand doesn't mean I was going to pour it in the punch at the prom."

He raised a skeptical brow.

"I was keeping a friend of mine from pouring it in the punch," she explained. "Not that anyone will believe me."

"As alibis go, I've heard better," he said.

"Anyway, I've been expelled and I won't graduate with my class and I'll have to go to summer school to finish. I'd rather run away from home than face Zach and Rebecca and tell them what I've done. In fact, the more I think about it, the better that idea sounds. I won't go home. I'll . . . I'll . . ."

"Go where?"

"I don't know. Somewhere."

"Dressed like that?"

She looked down at herself and back up at him, her eyes brimming with tears. "My dress is ruined. Just like my life."

Billy didn't resist the urge to lift her into his lap, and for whatever reason, she didn't resist his efforts to comfort her. She wrapped her arms around his neck and clung to him.

"I feel so lost and alone," she said, her breath moist against his skin. "I don't belong anywhere."

Billy tightened his arms around her protectively, wishing there was something more he could do to help. He crooned to her in Comanche, telling her she was safe, that he would find a way to help her, that she wasn't alone.

"What am I going to do?" she murmured in an anguished voice. "Where can I go?"

Billy swallowed over the knot in his throat. "You're going to think I'm crazy," he said. "But I've got an idea if you'd like to hear it."

"What is it?" she asked.

"You could come and live with me."

Two

Cherry had felt safe and secure in Billy Stonecreek's arms, that is, until he made his insane suggestion. She lifted her head from Billy's shoulder and stared at him wide-eyed. "What did you say?"

"Don't reject the idea before you hear me out."

"I'm listening." In fact, Cherry was fascinated.

He focused his dark-eyed gaze on her, pinning her in place. "The older lady who's been taking care of my kids is quitting on Monday. How would you like to work for me? The job comes with room and board." He smiled. "In fact, I'm including room and board because I can't afford to pay much."

"You're offering me a job?"

"And a place to live. I could be at home evenings to watch the girls while you go to night school over the summer and earn your high school diploma. What do you say?"

Cherry edged herself off Billy's lap, wondering how he had coaxed her into remaining there so long. Perversely, she missed the warmth of his embrace once it was gone. She pulled her knees up to her chest and wrapped her arms around the yards of pale green chiffon.

"Cherry?"

Her first reaction was to say yes. His offer was the simple solution to all her problems. She wouldn't have to go home. She wouldn't have to face her parents with the truth.

But she hadn't lived with Zach and Rebecca Whitelaw for four years and not learned how they felt about certain subjects. "My dad would never allow it."

"A minute ago you were going to run away from home. How is this different?"

"You obviously don't know Zach Whitelaw very well," she said with a rueful twist of her lips. "If he knew I was working so close, he'd expect me to live at home."

"Not if you were indispensible to me."

"Would I be?" she asked, intrigued.

"I can't manage the ranch and my six-year-old twin daughters all by myself. I'm up and working before dawn. Somebody has to make sure Annie and Rae-jean get dressed for school and feed them breakfast and be there when they get off the school bus in the afternoon." Billy shrugged. "You need a place to stay. I need help in a hurry. It's a match made in heaven."

Cherry shook her head. "It wouldn't work."

"Why not?"

"Can I be blunt?"

Billy smiled, and her stomach did a queer flip-flop. "By all means," he said.

"It's bad enough that you're single—"

"I wouldn't need the help if I had a wife," Billy interrupted.

Cherry frowned him into silence. "You're a wid-ower. I'm only eighteen. It's a toss-up which of us has the worse reputation for getting into trouble. Can you imagine what people would say—about us—if I moved in with you?" Cherry's lips curled in an imp-ish grin. "Eyebrows would hit hairlines all over the county."

Billy shook his head and laughed. "I hadn't thought about what people would think. We're two of a kind, all right." His features sobered. "Just not the right kind."

Cherry laid her hand on his arm in comfort. "I know what you're feeling, Billy."

"I doubt it."

Cherry felt bereft as he pulled free. He was wrong. She understood exactly what he was feeling. The words spilled out before she could stop them.

"Nobody wants anything to do with you, because you're different," she said in a quiet voice that carried in the dark. "To prove it doesn't matter what anyone else thinks, you break their rules. When they look down their noses at you, you spit in their eyes. And all the time, your heart is aching. Because you want them to like you. And respect you. But they don't."

Billy eyed her speculatively. "I guess you do understand."

For a moment Cherry thought he was going to put his arm around her. But he didn't.

She turned to stare at the pond, so he wouldn't see how much she regretted his decision to keep his distance. "I've always hated being different," she said. "I was always taller than everyone else, thanks to my giant of a father, Big Mike Murphy." When she was a child, her father's size had always made her feel safe. But he hadn't kept her safe. He had let her be stolen away from him.

"And I don't know another person with hair as godawful fire-engine red as mine. I have Big Mike to thank for that, too." Cherry noticed Billy didn't contradict her evaluation of her hair.

"And your mother?" Billy asked. "What did you get from her?"

"Nothing, so far as I can tell," Cherry said curtly. "She walked out on Big Mike when I was five. That's when he started drinking. Eventually someone reported to social services that he was leaving me alone at night. They took me away from him when I was eight. He fell from a high scaffolding at work the next week and was killed. I think he wanted to die. I was in and out of the system for six years before the Whitelaws took me in."

"I'm sorry."

"It doesn't matter now."

"Doesn't it?" Billy asked.

Cherry shrugged. "It's in the past. You learn to protect yourself."

"Yeah," Billy said. "You do."

Billy had inherited his six-foot-four height and dark brown eyes from his Scots father. His straight black hair and burnished skin came from his Comanche mother. They had been killed in a car wreck when he was ten. He had developed his rebellious streak in a series of foster homes that treated him like he was less than human because he wasn't all white.

He opened his mouth to share his common experiences with Cherry and closed it again. It was really none of her business.

"Too bad you aren't looking for a wife," Cherry mused. "That would solve your problem. But I guess after what happened, you don't want to get married again."

"No, I don't," Billy said flatly.

"I certainly wasn't volunteering for the job," Cherry retorted. Everyone knew Billy Stonecreek had made his first wife so unhappy she had killed herself. At least, that was the story Penelope Trask had been spreading. On the other hand, Billy Stonecreek had been nothing but nice to her. She couldn't help wondering whether Billy was really as villainous as his mother-in-law had painted him.

They sat in silence. Cherry wished there was some way she could have helped Billy. But she knew Zach Whitelaw too well to believe he would allow his daughter to move in with a single man—even if she was his housekeeper. Not that Zach could have stopped her if she wanted to do it. But knowing Zach, he would find a way to make sure Billy changed his mind about needing her. And she didn't want to cause that kind of trouble for anybody.

"Having you come to work for me wouldn't really solve my biggest problem, anyway," Billy said, picking up the beer can again.

Cherry took it out of his hand, set it down, and asked, "What problem is that?"

He hesitated so long she wasn't sure he was going to speak. At last he said, "My former mother-in-law is taking me to court to try and get custody of my daughters. Penelope says I'm not a fit parent. She's determined to take Raejean and Annie away from me."

"Oh, no!" It was Cherry's worst nightmare come to life. She had suffered terribly when she had been taken from her father as a child. "You can't let her do that! Kids belong with their parents."

Cherry was passionate about the subject. She had often wondered where her birth mother was and why she had walked away and left Cherry and Big Mike behind. Cherry had died inside when the social worker came to take her away, and she realized she was never going to see Big Mike again. It was outrageous to think someone could go to court and wrench two little girls away from their natural father.

"You've got to stop Mrs. Trask!" Cherry said. "You can't let her take your kids!"

"I'm not *letting* her do anything!" Billy cried in frustration. His hands clenched into fists. "But I'm not sure I can stop her. Over the past year I haven't exactly been a model citizen. And I haven't been able to keep a steady housekeeper. Especially once Penelope fills their ears with wild stories about me."

Billy made an angry sound in his throat. "If Laura hadn't died... Having a wife would certainly make my case as a responsible parent stronger in court."

"Isn't there somebody you could marry?"

"What woman would want a half-breed, with a ready-made family of half-breed kids?" Billy said bitterly.

Cherry gasped. "You talk like there's something wrong with you because you're part Comanche. I'm sure you have lots of redeeming qualities."

Billy eyed her sideways. "Like what?"

"I don't know. I'm sure there must be some." She paused and asked, "Aren't there?"

Billy snorted. "I've been in jail for fighting three times over the past year."

Cherry met his gaze evenly and said, "Nobody says you have to fight."

"True," Billy conceded. "But sometimes . . ."

"Sometimes you feel like if you don't hit something you'll explode?"

Billy nodded. "Yeah."

"I've felt that way sometimes myself."

"You're a girl," Billy protested. "Girls don't—"

"What makes you think girls don't get angry?" Cherry interrupted.

"I guess I never really thought much about it. What do you do when you feel like that?"

"Cause mischief," Cherry admitted with a grin. Her grin faded as she said, "Think, Billy. Isn't there some woman you could ask to marry you?"

Billy shook his head. "I haven't gone out much since Laura died. When I haven't been working on the ranch, I've spent my time with Raejean and Annie. Besides, I don't know too many women around here who'd think I was much of a catch."

Cherry sat silently beside Billy. Her heart went out to his two daughters. She knew what was coming for them. She felt genuinely sorry for them. For the first time in a long time she regretted her past behavior, because it meant she couldn't be a help to them.

"I wish we'd met sooner. And that I had less of a reputation for being a troublemaker," Cherry said. "If things were different, I might volunteer to help you out. But I'm not the kind of person you'd want as a mother for your kids."

Billy's head jerked around, and he stared intently at her.

Cherry was a little frightened by the fierce look on his face. "Billy? What are you thinking?"

"Why not?" he muttered. "Why the hell not?"

"Why not what?"

"Why can't you marry me?" Billy said.

Cherry clutched at her torn bodice as she surged to her feet. "You can't be serious!"

Billy rose and grabbed her by the shoulders, which was all that kept her from running. "More serious than I've ever been in my life. My kids' lives depend on me making the right choices now."

"And you think marriage to me is the right choice?" Cherry asked incredulously. "We're practically strangers! I barely know you. You don't know me at all."

"I know plenty about you. You understand what it feels like to be different. What it feels like to lose your parents. What it feels like to need a parent's love. You'd be good for my kids. And you could really help me out."

"Why me?"

"I'm desperate," Billy said. "I thought you were, too."

Cherry grimaced. Why else would a man choose her except because he was desperate? And why else would a woman accept such a proposal, unless she were desperate, too?

"Are you ready to go home and face your parents and tell them you got expelled and that you aren't going to graduate?" Billy demanded.

"When you put it that way, I... No. But marriage? That seems like such a big step. Make that a *huge* step."

"It doesn't have to be a real marriage. It can be strictly a business arrangement. We can stay married long enough for you to finish the high school credits you need and maybe take some courses at the junior college. When you figure out what you want to do with the rest of your life, we could go our separate ways."

"Couldn't I just be your housekeeper?"

Billy shook his head. "You've said yourself why that wouldn't work."

"But marriage is so... permanent."

"It would be if it were for real. Ours wouldn't be."

"Are you suggesting we tell people we're married but not really go through with it?"

He considered a moment. "No, we'd have to get married, and as far as I'm concerned, the sooner the better."

Cherry's heart bounced around inside her like a frightened rabbit. She pressed a fistful of chiffon hard against her chest, as though she could hold her heart still, but it kept right on jumping. "You want to get married right away? This week?"

"As soon as we can. We could fly to Las Vegas tonight."

"Fly?"

"I've got a pilot's license. We can charter a small private plane for the trip. Would you mind?"

"I guess not," Cherry said, overwhelmed by the speed at which things were moving.

"The more I think about it, the more I like the whole idea. Getting married would certainly spike Penelope's guns."

Cherry gnawed on her lower lip. "If you're looking for someone who'd be an asset in court, maybe you ought to reconsider taking me as your wife. My reputation's almost as bad as yours."

"You're a Whitelaw," Billy said. "That means something around this part of Texas."

"An adopted Whitelaw," Cherry reminded him. "And I'm not so sure my parents wouldn't change their minds if they had the chance."

Billy smiled. "I think we can make this arrangement work for both of us. How about it, Cherry? Will you marry me?"

If Cherry had been anybody except who she was, she would have said no. Any rational person would have. It didn't make sense to marry a virtual stranger, one who had reportedly made his previous wife miserable. But Cherry wasn't thinking about Billy or even about herself. She was thinking about his two innocent little girls. If marrying Billy would give them a better chance of staying with their father, she really didn't think she had any other choice.

"All right, Billy," she said. "I'll marry you."

Billy gave a whoop of joy, swept her up into his arms, and whirled her in a dizzying circle, sending chiffon flying around her.

"Put me down, Billy," she said, laughing.

He immediately set her on her feet. When she swayed dizzily, he reached out to steady her.

The feel of his strong, callused hands on her bare shoulders sent an unexpected quiver skittering down her spine. She knew she ought to step away, but Billy's dark eyes held her spellbound.

"Okay now?" he asked, his voice rasping over her.

"I'm fine." She shivered, belying her words.

"You must be getting chilly." He slipped an arm around her shoulder that was warm and supportive...and possessive.

She shivered again as he began walking her toward his pickup. Only this time she realized it had nothing to do with the cold.

As Billy held open the pickup door she said as casually as she could, "This will be a marriage in name only, right?"

He closed the door behind her, slid over the hood, got into the cab, and started the pickup before he answered, "That's right."

She gave a gusty sigh of relief as the engine roared to life. "Good."

"We don't even have to sleep in the same bed," Billy said as he headed back toward the main road. "You can have the room my housekeeper will be vacating. If I feel the urge for some feminine comfort, I can get what I need from a woman in town."

"Wait a minute," Cherry said. "I don't think I'm going to want my husband satisfying his lustful urges in town."

"I won't really be your husband," Billy reminded her.

"As far as my parents and neighbors and friends are concerned, you will be."

Billy eyed her cautiously. "What do you suggest?"

"Couldn't you just... not do it."

"I'm a man, not a monk," Billy said.

Cherry pursed her lips thoughtfully. "Then I suppose I'd rather you come to me than go to some other woman."

"This is starting to sound like a real marriage," Billy said suspiciously. "I was looking for a temporary solution to both our problems."

"Oh, you don't have to worry about me falling in love with you or anything," Cherry reassured him. "I don't believe in happily-ever-after."

"You don't?"

Cherry shook her head. "Except for the Whitelaws, I've never met any married couples who really loved each other. But I can see where it would be unfair to expect you to give up sex for who knows how long. Only, if you don't mind, I'd rather we had a chance to get to know each other a little better before...you know..."

"Maybe this marriage thing isn't such a good idea, after all," Billy said. "You're just a kid, and—"

"I may be only eighteen," Cherry interrupted, "but I've lived a lifetime since my father died. You don't have to worry about me. I've been in and out of a dozen foster homes. I've spent time in juvenile detention. I've survived the past four years in a house with seven other adopted brothers and sisters. I've come through it all with a pretty good idea of what I want from life. I'm plenty old enough to know exactly what I'm doing."

"I doubt that," Billy said. Maybe if he hadn't been so panicked at the thought of losing Annie and Raejean, he would have taken more time to think the matter over. But marriage to Cherry Whitelaw would solve so many problems all at once, he accepted her statement at face value.

"All right, Cherry. We'll do this your way. I won't go looking for comfort in town, and you'll provide for my needs at home."

"After we get to know one another," Cherry qualified.

"After we get to know one another," Billy agreed.

He turned onto the main highway and headed for the airport. "Will your parents worry if you don't show up at home tonight?"

"It's prom night. I was supposed to be staying out all night with some friends of mine and have breakfast with them tomorrow. In fact, if you'll stop by my friend's house, I've got an overnight bag there with a change of clothes."

"Good. That'll leave us about twelve hours to get to Las Vegas and tie the knot before we have to face your parents."

Cherry pictured that meeting in her mind. *Good grief,* she thought. *The fur is going to fly.*

Three

The wedding chapel in Las Vegas was brightly lit, even at 3:00 a.m. To Cherry's amazement, they weren't the only couple getting married at such an ungodly hour. She and Billy had to wait ten minutes for an elderly couple to complete their vows before it was their turn. The longer they waited, the more second thoughts she had. What had she been thinking? Zach was going to be furious. Rebecca was going to cry.

The image she conjured of two identical cherubic six-year-old faces was all that kept her from running for a phone to call Zach and Rebecca to come get her. She tried to recall what Billy's twins looked like from the last time she had seen them at church. All she could remember were large dark eyes—like Billy's, she realized now—in small, round faces.

What qualities had they gotten from their mother? Cherry tried to remember how Laura Trask had looked the few times she had seen her. Did the twins have delicate noses like hers? Determined chins? Bowed lips? Had they remained petite like their mother, or become tall and raw-boned like their father?

"If you keep chewing on your lip like that, you're going to gnaw it right off."

Startled, Cherry let go of her lower lip and turned to find Billy behind her.

"Here," he said, handing her a bouquet of gardenias. "I got them from a vendor out in front of the chapel. I thought you might like to carry some flowers."

"Thank you, Billy." Cherry took the bouquet with a hand that shook. "I guess I'm a little nervous."

"Me, too," he admitted.

Cherry wished he would smile. He didn't.

"The bouquet was a lovely thought." She raised it to her nose and sniffed. And sneezed. And sneezed again. "I must be—*achoo!*"

"Allergic," Billy finished, the smile appearing as he retrieved the bouquet from her and set it on an empty folding chair. "Forget the flowers. There are blooms enough in your cheeks for me."

"You mean the freckles," Cherry said, covering her cheeks with her hands. "I know they're awful, but—"

Billy took her hands in his and kissed her gently on each cheek. "They're tasty bits of brown sugar. Didn't anyone ever tell you that?"

Cherry froze as a memory of long ago came to mind. She was sitting on Big Mike's lap at the supper table. He was alternately taking bites of vanilla ice cream and giving her ice-cold kisses across her nose and cheeks, making yummy sounds in his throat and saying, "Your freckles sure taste sweet, baby."

Her throat tightened with emotion, and she looked up, half expecting to see Big Mike standing in front of her.

But it was Billy, his brow furrowed as his dark eyes took in the pallor beneath her freckles. "Are you all right? You look like you're about to faint."

Cherry stiffened knees that were threatening to buckle. "I've never fainted in my life. I don't expect to start now."

"Are you folks ready?" the minister asked.

"Last chance to back out," Billy whispered to Cherry.

The sound tickled her ear, but she managed to stifle the inappropriate giggle that sought voice. This ridiculous wedding ceremony was serious business. "I'm not backing out. But if you've changed your mind—"

"I haven't," Billy interrupted her.

He tightened his grip on one of her hands and released the other, leading her down the aisle to the makeshift pulpit at the front of the room.

Throughout the ceremony, Cherry kept repeating two things over and over.

Those little girls need me. And, *This is the last time I'll be disappointing Zach and Rebecca. Once I'm married, I won't be their responsibility anymore.*

She was concentrating so hard on convincing herself she was doing the right thing that she had to be prompted to respond when the time came.

"Cherry?"

She turned and found Billy's eyes on her. Worried again. *And I won't be a burden to Billy Stonecreek, either,* she added for good measure. "What is it, Billy?"

"Your turn to say I do."

Cherry gave Billy a tremulous smile and said, "I do." It was more of a croak, actually, but when Billy smiled back, she knew it was all right.

"Rings?" the minister asked.

"We don't have any," Billy replied.

The minister pulled open a drawer in a credenza behind him, and she heard a tinny clatter. To Cherry's amazement, the drawer was full of fake gold rings.

"Help yourself," the minister said.

Cherry watched Billy select a plain yellow band and try it on her finger. Too small. The next was too big. The third was also a little loose, but because she wanted the awkward moment over with she said, "This one's fine, Billy."

"That'll be ten dollars extra," the minister said.

She saw the annoyed look that crossed Billy's face and pulled the ring off. "I don't need a ring."

Billy caught it before it could drop into the drawer and put it back on her finger. He caught her chin and lifted it so she was forced to look at him. "I'm sorry, Cherry. I should have thought of getting you a ring. This is so..."

Cheap? Tawdry? Vulgar? Cherry knew what he was thinking, but couldn't bring herself to say it, either. "Don't worry about it, Billy. It doesn't matter."

"You deserve better."

"It's not a real marriage. I don't need a real ring," Cherry said quietly so the minister wouldn't overhear.

Billy let go of her chin. He opened his mouth as though to speak and closed it again. Finally he said, "I guess you're right. This one will have to do. Shall we get this over with?"

They turned back to the minister, and he finished the ceremony. "You may kiss the bride," the minister said at last.

It wasn't a real wedding, so Cherry wasn't expecting a real kiss. To her surprise, Billy put his hands on either side of her face and murmured, "The ring is phony, but at least this can be real."

Cherry had done her share of kissing. Experimenting with sex was an age-old method of teenage rebellion. She thought she knew everything there was to know about kissing and sex. It was no big deal. Boys seemed to like it a lot, but she didn't understand what all the fuss was about.

Something odd happened when Billy Stonecreek's lips feathered across hers. An unexpected curl of desire flitted across her belly and shot up to her breasts. Her hands clutched fistfuls of his Western shirt as his mouth settled firmly over hers. His tongue traced the seam of her closed lips, causing them to tingle. She opened her mouth, and his tongue slipped inside for a quick taste of her.

She made a sound in her throat somewhere between confusion and protest.

His hand slid around to capture her nape and keep her from escaping.

Cherry wasn't going anywhere. She was enthralled by what Billy was doing with his lips and teeth and tongue. She had never felt anything remotely like it. Before she was ready, the kiss ended.

She stared, bemused, into Billy's hooded eyes. His lips were still damp from hers, and she didn't resist the impulse to reach out and touch.

His hand clamped around her wrist like a vise as her fingertips caressed his lips. "Don't." His voice was harsh, and his lips pressed flat in irritation.

Cherry realized her reaction, her naive curiosity, must have embarrassed him. The kiss had merely been a token of thanks from Billy. He didn't want anything from her in return.

She had told him she didn't want to be touched until they knew each other better. But she had touched him. She had set the ground rules, and then she hadn't followed them.

It wasn't a real marriage. She had to remember that.

There were papers to sign and collect before they could leave. The minister was in a hurry, because two more couples had arrived and were awaiting their turns. Minutes after the ceremony ended, she and Billy were back in the rental car they had picked up at the airport.

Billy finally broke the uncomfortable silence that had fallen between them. "I don't know about you, but I could use a few hours of sleep before we fly back. We have the time. Your parents won't start missing you until noon."

"I must admit I feel exhausted," Cherry said. But she wasn't sure whether it was fatigue or a delayed reaction to their strange wedding. She had never wanted to get married, but that didn't mean she hadn't fantasized about having a grand wedding. She had imagined wearing a white satin gown with a train twenty feet long, having at least three bridesmaids, and hearing the wedding processional played on an immense pipe organ. This ceremony had fallen far short of the fantasy.

"Regrets?" Billy asked.

Cherry stared at him, surprised at his intuitiveness. "Were my thoughts that transparent?"

"I can't imagine any woman wanting to get married the way we did. But drastic situations sometimes require drastic solutions. In this case I believe the end—we're now legally husband and wife—justifies the means."

Cherry hoped Zach would see the logic in such an argument.

The hotel Billy chose was outlined in pink and white neon and advertised a honeymoon suite in the center of a pink neon heart. "At least we're sure they've got a honeymoon suite here," Billy said with a cheeky grin.

Cherry laughed breathlessly. "Why would we need a honeymoon suite?"

"It's probably going to have a bigger bed than the other rooms," Billy said. "It'll be more comfortable for someone my size."

"Oh," Cherry said.

"That almost sounded like disappointment," Billy said. "I agreed to wait until you're ready to make it a real marriage. Are you telling me you're ready?"

"No, Billy. I'm not."

He didn't say anything.

"Are you disappointed?" Cherry asked.

"I guess grooms have fantasies about their wedding nights the way brides have fantasies about their weddings," Billy conceded with a grin. "Yeah. I suppose I am. But I'll survive."

Cherry wondered if Billy was remembering his first wedding night. She knew she looked nothing like Laura Trask. She wasn't the least bit petite. Her hair wasn't golden blond, and she didn't move with stately grace. She had a million freckles that speckled her milk-white skin and frizzy hair that changed color depending on the way the sun struck it. She had a small bosom that had no freckles at all and absolutely no intention of letting the groom find that out for himself tonight. No, this was not a night for fulfilling fantasies.

She followed Billy inside the hotel with the overnight bag she had picked up at her friend's house, so they weren't entirely without luggage. She pressed the ring tight against her fourth finger with her thumb so it wouldn't slip off. She stood at Billy's shoulder while he registered and got a key card for the door.

They took the elevator to the top floor and found the honeymoon suite at the end of the hall. Billy used the key card to open the door.

Before she could say anything, Billy picked her up and carried her over the threshold. She was wearing the jeans and T-shirt she had put on to replace the torn chiffon dress and she could feel the heat of him everywhere his body touched hers.

Her arm automatically clutched at his shoulder to help him support her weight, but she realized when she felt the corded muscles there, that he didn't need any help. He carried her over to the bed and let her drop.

She bounced a couple of times and came to rest. "Good grief," she said, staring at the heart-shaped bed. "How do they expect two people to sleep on something shaped like this?"

He wiggled his eyebrows. "I don't think they expect you to sleep, if you know what I mean." He dropped onto the bed beside her and stretched out on his back with his hands behind his head on one of the pillows. "It's nowhere near as big as it looked in neon, either."

Cherry scooted as far from him as she could, but although there was plenty of room for two pillows at the top of the bed, the bottom narrowed so their feet ended up nearly touching.

Billy toed off one cowboy boot, then used his stockinged foot to shove off the other boot. He reached for the phone beside the bed. "I'll ask for an eight o'clock wake-up call," he said. "That'll give us time to fly back before noon."

Cherry was wearing tennis shoes, and she reached down and tugged them off with her hands and dropped them on the floor. She lay back on the pillow with her legs as far on her side of the bed as she could get them, which was a few bare inches from Billy's feet.

Billy reached over and turned out the lamp beside the bed. It should have been dark in the room, but the neon lights outside bathed the room in a romantic pink glow.

"Do you want me to close the curtains?" Billy asked.

"It's kind of pretty."

Which might make a difference if they wanted to watch each other while they made love, Cherry thought, but wasn't going to matter much when they closed their eyes to sleep. But she noticed Billy didn't get up to close the curtains.

"Good night, Cherry," Billy said, turning on his side away from her. "Thanks again."

"Good night, Billy," Cherry said, turning on her side away from him. "You're welcome."

She lay there in uncomfortable silence for perhaps five minutes before she whispered, "Are you asleep, Billy?"

Cherry felt the bed dip as he turned back toward her.

"I thought you were tired," he said.

"I am. But I'm too excited to sleep. It's not every day a girl gets married."

She stiffened when she felt one of his hands touch her shoulder and slide down to the small of her back.

"Don't get skittish on me, woman. I'm just going to rub your back a little to help you relax."

His thumb hit her somewhere in the center of her back, and his hand wrapped around her side.

Cherry gave a luxuriant sigh as he massaged her tense muscles.

"Feel better?"

"Yes." She was impressed again by his strength. And his gentleness. And wondered how his hand would feel caressing other places on her body.

Cherry sought a subject they could discuss that would get her mind off the direction it seemed to be headed. "Could you tell me a little bit about your daughters?"

"Raejean and Annie are just finishing the first grade. Their teacher has had a devil of a time telling them apart."

"Do they look that much alike?" Cherry asked.

Billy chuckled. "Sometimes they try to fool me. But it isn't hard to tell them apart once you get to know them. Raejean carries herself differently, more confidently. She looks at you more directly and talks back more often. Annie is kinder, sweeter, more thoughtful. She follows Raejean's lead. When the two of them team up, they can be a handful."

"Have you had a lot of trouble with them?"

His hand paused for a moment, then resumed its disturbing massage. "A little. Just lately. I think they're missing Laura as much as I am."

He rubbed a little harder, as though he had admitted something he wished he hadn't.

"Were you expecting twins when they were born?"

Cherry felt his hand tighten uncomfortably on her flesh. She hissed in a breath, and his hand soothed the hurt.

"The twins were a complete surprise. They came early, and for a while it was touch and go whether Laura and the girls would all make it. They did, but there were complications. The doctor said Laura couldn't have any more children."

"You wanted more?"

"I didn't care one way or the other. But Laura did."

Abruptly his hand left her back, and he rolled away from her. "Go to sleep, Cherry."

Apparently their conversation was over, leaving her with a great deal of food for thought.

The twins missed their mother. Like he did.

Cherry could do something to replace the loss in the twins' lives. She could be a mother to Billy's little girls. Of more concern was the temptation she felt to ease Billy's sorrow. There were dangers in such an undertaking. She had to remember this was a temporary marriage. It was safer to let Billy cope with his loss on his own.

On the other hand, Cherry never had chosen the safe path. As she closed her eyes again, she saw the four of them smiling at one another...one happy family.

Billy stared at the neon outside the window, willing himself to sleep. But he couldn't stop thinking about his new wife.

The wedding kiss had surprised him. In the fluorescent light of the wedding chapel, Cherry Whitelaw had looked like anything but a radiant bride. Her blue eyes had been wide with fright and her skin pale beneath a mass of orange freckles. He'd had significant second thoughts about the marriage. And third and fourth thoughts, as well. All his thoughts came back to the same thing. She needed his help. And he needed hers.

He had been proud of her for getting through that awful ceremony—including the last-minute search for a ring that would fit—with so much dignity. That was why he had offered her the kiss, not because he had been wondering what her lips would taste like. When she had reached out to him afterward, he had stopped her because that wasn't part of their deal, not because he had been shocked at the way his body had gone rock-hard at her touch. Just thinking about it caused the same reaction all over again.

Billy swore.

"Billy? Is something wrong?"

''Nothing's wrong, Cherry. Go to sleep.''

He closed his eyes, determined to get some rest, but a picture of her breast half revealed by the torn chiffon bodice appeared behind his eyelids.

He opened his eyes and stared at the neon again. Who would have thought he would find a freckle-faced redhead so erotically exciting? Or that his new wife would be off-limits for heaven knew how long? Billy heaved a long-suffering sigh. It was going to be one hell of a marriage.

His eyes slid closed again as sleep claimed his exhausted body.

Billy was having a really spectacular dream. He had a handful of soft female breast, which just happened to belong to his new wife. Her eyes were closed in passion, and as he flicked his thumb across her nipple, he heard a moan that made his loins tighten. He lowered his head to take her nipple in his mouth. It was covered by a thin layer of cotton. He sucked on her through the damp cloth and felt her body arch toward him. Her hands threaded into his hair... and yanked on it—

Billy came awake with a jerk. ''What the hell?''

Cherry was sitting bolt upright in bed with her hands crossed defensively under her breasts. A damp spot on her T-shirt revealed that he hadn't been dreaming.

It shouldn't have surprised him. His last thoughts before drifting to sleep had been about Cherry. No wonder his body had been drawn to hers during the night. He shoved a hand through hair that was standing on end and groaned. "God, Cherry, I'm sorry. I was dreaming."

She eyed him suspiciously.

"I swear I didn't know what I was doing."

That made her look crestfallen.

"Not that it isn't exactly what I'd like to be doing at this moment," he said.

She gave a hitching breath that was almost a sob. "We agreed to wait."

"Yeah, I know," Billy said. "I don't suppose you've changed your mind."

She hesitated so long he thought maybe she had. Until she shook her head no.

Billy looked at the clock. It was only six. But he didn't trust himself to lie back down beside her. "I can't sleep anymore. How about if we head for the airport?"

"All right," she said.

He started pulling on his boots and felt her hand on his shoulder. He froze.

She cleared her throat and said, "I liked what you were doing, Billy. It felt . . . good. I wanted you to know that. It's just . . ."

He shoved his foot down into the boot and stood. He had to get away from her or he was going to turn around and lay her flat on the bed and do something he would be sorry for later. "I know," he said. "We agreed to wait."

She had a brave smile on her face. And looked every bit her youthful age.

What on earth had possessed him to marry her?

It was a silent flight from Las Vegas to the airport in Amarillo. And an even more silent truck ride to the Stonecreek Ranch. Billy pulled up to the back door of a large, two-story white clapboard house and killed the engine. The blue morning glories he had planted for Laura were soaking up the midday sun on a trellis along the eastern edge of the porch.

"We're home," Billy said. His throat tightened painfully. They were the same words he had spoken to Laura—how many years ago?—when they had moved into this house.

Suddenly he realized he couldn't go back into Laura's house right now with a new wife. It was still too full of Laura. He needed a little time to accept the fact that she really was gone forever.

"Look, why don't you go inside and introduce yourself to Mrs. Motherwell, my housekeeper. I just realized I was supposed to pick up a load of feed in town this morning. I'll be back in an hour or so."

Cherry was staring at him as if he had grown a second head. "You want me to go in there without you?" she asked.

"Just tell Mrs. Motherwell you've come to replace her. I'll explain everything to the kids when I get back." When Cherry continued sitting there staring at him, he snapped, "Changed your mind already?"

His new wife looked sober and thoughtful. There were shadows of fatigue beneath her eyes. "No. I'm determined to see this through." She gave him one last anxious look before she left the truck. "Don't be gone long."

"I won't."

Billy resisted the urge to gun the engine as he backed away from the house. Once he hit paved road he headed the truck toward town. He hadn't gone two miles when he saw flashing red and blue lights behind him. He glanced down at the speedometer and swore. He swerved off the road and braked hard enough to raise a cloud of dust.

He was out of the truck and reaching for his wallet to get his driver's license when he saw the highway patrolman had a gun in his hand that was pointed at him.

"Freeze, Stonecreek, or I'll blow your head off."

Billy froze. "What the hell's the matter with you?"

"Put your hands up. You're under arrest."

"Arrest? For what?"

"Kidnapping."

It took a full second for the charge to register. *Kidnapping?* Then he realized what must have happened and groaned. "Look, Officer, I can explain everything."

"You have the right to remain silent," the officer began.

Billy's lips pressed flat. He had married Cherry Whitelaw in the hope of solving his problems. Instead he had jumped right out of the frying pan into the fire.

Four

Cherry stared at the back door of Billy's house—now her home, too—trying to work up the courage to go inside, wondering, absurdly, if she should knock first.

She turned and stole a glance at Billy's rugged profile as he drove away, pondering what it was about him she had found so beguiling. He had rescued her, listened to her troubles, and shared his in return. She had felt his desperation and responded to it. Now he was her husband. She twisted the cheap gold ring that confirmed it wasn't all a dream, that she was, indeed, Mrs. Billy Stonecreek.

Good grief. What had she done?

Cherry had gone off half-cocked in the past, but the enormity of this escapade was finally sinking in. Surely it would have been better to face Zach and Rebecca and explain the truth of what had happened at the dance. How was she going to justify this latest lapse of common sense?

She felt a surge of anger at Billy for abandoning her at the door. It wouldn't have taken long to introduce her to Mrs. Motherwell and explain the situation. So why hadn't he done it?

Maybe because he's having the same second thoughts as you are. Maybe in the cold light of day he's thinking he made a bad bargain. Maybe he's trying to figure out a way right now to get out of it.

If the back door hadn't opened at that precise moment, Cherry would have turned and headed for Hawk's Pride.

But it did. And Cherry found herself face-to-face with Penelope Trask.

"I saw you standing out here," Mrs. Trask said. "Is there something I can do for you?"

"I, uh . . . Is Mrs. Motherwell here?"

"She packed her bags and left this morning."

Cherry stood with her jaw agape, speechless for perhaps the first time in her life. Had Mrs. Trask already managed to gain legal custody of Billy's children? Had their marriage been for naught? She wished Billy were here.

"Don't I know you? Aren't you one of those Whitelaw Bra—" Mrs. Trask cut herself off.

Cherry knew what she had been about to say. The eight adopted Whitelaw kids were known around this part of Texas as the Whitelaw Brats, just like Zach and his siblings before them, and Grandpa Garth and his siblings before that. Cherry had done her share to help earn the nickname. She was proud to be one of them.

She met the older woman's disdainful look with defiance. "Yes, I'm a Whitelaw Brat. You have a problem with that?"

"None at all. But if you're looking for your missing sister, she isn't here. I have no idea what my no-account excuse for a son-in-law has done with her." She started to close the door in Cherry's face.

Cherry stuck her foot in the door. "Wait! What are you talking about?"

A flare of recognition lit Mrs. Trask's eyes. "Oh, my God. You're the girl, aren't you? The one Billy kidnapped." She stuck her head out the screen door and looked around. "Where is he? I have a few things to say to him."

"Kidnapped?" Cherry gasped. "I wasn't kidnapped!"

"Your parents reported you missing late last night."

"Why would they think I was with Billy?"

"Your date wrapped his car around a telephone pole, and when he kept mumbling your name the police called your parents, thinking maybe you'd been thrown from the car. At the hospital, the boy told your father that he'd left you at the stock pond with Billy, after my son-in-law ran him off with his fists.

"Your father couldn't find you at the stock pond, and when he came looking for you here in a rage, Mrs. Motherwell called me. Your father seemed bent on strangling someone before the night was out."

Probably me, Cherry thought morosely.

"Of course I came right over," Mrs. Trask said. "All I could tell your father was that I wouldn't put it past my reckless son-in-law to kidnap an innocent young woman."

"Mrs. Trask, I wasn't kidnapped."

"I suggest you go home and tell that to your father. He told the police Billy must have kidnapped you, because you'd never go off on your own like that." Mrs. Trask smirked. "Of course, that was before he found out you'd been expelled from school earlier in the evening."

Cherry groaned.

"You're in an awful lot of trouble, young lady. Where have you been? And where's Billy?"

Cherry put a hand to her throbbing temple. Zach and Rebecca must be frantic with worry. And disappointed beyond belief. She didn't want to think about how angry they were going to be when they heard what she had done.

"May I please use your phone?" It was her phone now, so she shouldn't have to ask. Except, this didn't seem the right moment to announce that she and Billy had run off to Las Vegas to get married.

Mrs. Trask hesitated, then pushed the screen door open wide. "Come on in, if you must."

As soon as Cherry's eyes adjusted to the dim light in the kitchen, she saw Raejean and Annie standing together near the table.

They wore their straight black hair in adorable, beribboned pigtails, and stared at her with dark, serious brown eyes. Their noses were small and their chins dainty, like their mother, but they had high, sharp cheekbones that reminded her of Billy. They were tall for six-year-olds and dressed exactly alike in collared blouses tucked into denim coveralls and white tennis shoes.

"Hello, Raejean," she said, addressing the child who had her arm wrapped comfortingly around the other's shoulder.

The child's eyes widened in surprise at being recognized. Then she said, "I'm not Raejean, I'm Annie."

The other twin's mouth dropped open, and she glanced at her sister. Then she turned to Cherry, pointed to her chest with her thumb, and said, "I'm Raejean."

"I see," Cherry said. They were both missing the exact same front tooth. No help there telling them apart. Billy had said Raejean was the confident one, so Cherry had assumed it was Raejean who was giving comfort to her sister. But maybe she had been wrong.

"I need to use your phone," she said, moving toward where it hung on the kitchen wall.

Cherry felt the girls watching her while she dialed.

"We don't need another housekeeper," the twin who had identified herself as Annie said. "We're going to stay at Nana's house until Daddy gets home."

Cherry felt her heart miss a beat. She turned to Mrs. Trask and said, "Billy went into town for supplies. He should be back any time now. There's no need to take the girls anywhere."

"I'll be the best judge of that," Mrs. Trask said. "Go upstairs, girls, and finish packing."

The twins turned and ran. Cherry heard their footsteps pounding on the stairs as the ringing phone was answered by her sister, Jewel. Of her seven Whitelaw siblings, Jewel was the sister closest to her in age. Jewel had been adopted by Zach and Rebecca when she was five—the first of the current generation of Whitelaw Brats.

It had taken Cherry a while to straighten them all out, but now she could recite their names and ages with ease. Rolleen was 21, Jewel was 19, she was 18,

Avery was 17, Jake was 16, Frannie was 13, Rabbit was 12, and Colt was 11.

Of course Rabbit's name wasn't really Rabbit, it was Louis, but nobody called him that. Jewel had given him the nickname Rabbit when he was little, because he ate so many carrots, and the name had stuck. Colt was the only one of them who had been adopted as a baby. The rest of them had all known at least one other parent before being abandoned, orphaned, or fostered out.

"Is anybody there?" Jewel asked breathlessly. "If this is the kidnapper, we'll pay whatever you ask."

"It's me, Jewel."

"Cherry! Where are you? Are you all right? Are you hurt?"

"I'm fine. I'm at Billy Stonecreek's ranch."

"So he did kidnap you! I'll send Daddy to get you right away."

"No! I mean..." Cherry had turned her back to Mrs. Trask and kept her voice low thus far, but she figured there was no sense postponing the inevitable. "Billy didn't kidnap me. Last night we flew to Las Vegas and got married."

She was met with stunned silence on the other end of the line. Which was a good thing, because Mrs. Trask gave an outraged shriek that brought the two little girls back downstairs on the run.

"Nana! Nana! What's wrong?"

"I have to go now, Jewel," Cherry said. "Tell Zach and Rebecca I'm okay, and that I'll come to see them soon and explain everything."

"Cherry, don't—"

Cherry hung up the phone in time to turn and greet the twins a second time. Again, she identified the twin taking the lead as Raejean, which meant the one standing slightly behind her was Annie. "Hello, Raejean. Hello, Annie."

"I'm Annie," Raejean contradicted.

Before Annie could misidentify herself as Raejean, Mrs. Trask snapped, "Don't bother trying to tell them apart. They're identical, you know."

"But—" From Billy's descriptions of them it was so obvious to her which twin was which. Couldn't Mrs. Trask see the difference?

"What's wrong, Nana?" Raejean asked. "Why did you scream?"

Mrs. Trask's face looked more like a beet or a turnip than a human head, she was so flushed. It was clear she wasn't sure exactly what to say.

"Your grandmother was just excited about some news she heard," Cherry said.

"What news?" Annie asked.

"It's a surprise I think your Daddy will want to tell you about himself when he gets home," Cherry said.

"We're not going to be here that long," Mrs. Trask retorted. "The girls and I are leaving."

"Not until Billy gets back," Cherry said firmly. "I'm sure Raejean and Annie want to wait and say goodbye to their father." Cherry turned to the girls and asked, "Don't you?"

Raejean eyed her consideringly, but Annie piped up, "I want to wait for Daddy."

Mrs. Trask made an angry sound in her throat. "I hope you're happy now," she said to Cherry. "My grandchildren have had a difficult enough time over the past year, without adding someone like you to the picture."

Cherry reminded herself that Mrs. Trask was always going to be Raejean and Annie's grandmother. Throwing barbs now, however satisfying it might be, would only cause problems later. Zach and Rebecca would have been astounded at her tact when she spoke.

"I'm sorry we surprised you like this, Mrs. Trask. I know Billy will want to explain everything to you himself. Won't you consider waiting until he returns before you leave?"

"No."

Of course, there were times when being blunt worked best. Cherry crossed to stand beside the twins. "I'm sorry you have to leave, Mrs. Trask. The girls and I will have Billy give you a call when he gets home."

Cherry saw the moment when Mrs. Trask realized that she had been outmaneuvered. She wasn't going to make a quick and easy escape with Billy's children. Cherry was there to stand in her way.

Billy chose that moment to pull open the screen door and step into the kitchen.

Annie and Raejean gave shrieks of joy and raced into his wide open arms. He lifted them both, one in each arm, and gave them each a smacking kiss. "How are my girls?" he asked.

Raejean answered for both of them.

"Some man got mad at Mrs. Motherwell because she didn't know where you were and Nana came and Mrs. Motherwell packed her bags and left and Nana said we should pack, too, and go live with her until you came back home, only this lady came a little while ago and said you were coming home really soon and we had to wait for you because you have a surprise for us. What's our surprise, Daddy? Can we have it now?"

Cherry had watched Billy's narrowed gaze flicker from his daughter to Mrs. Trask and back again as Raejean made her breathless recital. When Raejean got to the part about a surprise, his gaze shot to her, and she thought she saw both panic and resignation.

"What are you doing back here so soon?" Mrs. Trask said. "I was told you were going into town for supplies."

"I got stopped by the police long before I got there and arrested for kidnapping," Billy said.

"Then why aren't you in jail?" Mrs. Trask demanded.

Billy's lips curled. "I showed them my marriage license."

"Who got kidnapped, Daddy?" Annie asked.

"Nobody, sweetheart," Billy replied. "It was all a big mistake."

"Then, can we have our surprise now?" Annie asked.

He knelt down and set them back on their feet. Keeping an arm around each of them, he said, "The surprise is that you have a new mother."

Annie's brow furrowed. "A new mother?"

Raejean frowned. "Our mother is in heaven."

"I know that," Billy said in a sandpaper-rough voice that made Cherry's throat swell with emotion. "I've married someone else who's going to be your mother from now on."

Raejean and Annie looked at each other, then turned as one to stare with shocked, suspicious eyes at Cherry.

Raejean's head shot around to confront her father. "Her?"

Billy nodded.

Raejean jerked free and shouted, "I don't want another mother! Make her go away!" Then she ran from the room.

Annie's eyes had filled with tears and one spilled over as she stared at Raejean's fleeing form. Cherry willed the softhearted child to accept her, but Annie paused only another moment before she turned and ran after her sister.

Cherry met Billy's stricken gaze. She felt sick to her stomach. The two charming and innocent little girls she had married Billy to save from harm, didn't want anything to do with her.

"You're a fool, Billy," Mrs. Trask said, grabbing her purse from the kitchen counter. "I don't know what you hoped to accomplish with this charade, but it won't work. I'm more convinced than ever that my grandchildren belong with me." She gave Cherry a look down her nose. "I'll see you both in court."

She made a grand exit through the doorway that led to the front of the house. Cherry and Billy stood unmoving until they heard the front door slam behind her.

"She's right," Billy said. "I always intend to do the right thing, but somehow it turns out wrong."

"This wasn't wrong, Billy. If I hadn't gotten here when I did, Mrs. Trask would have taken the children and been gone before you returned. At least Raejean and Annie are still here."

"And angry and unhappy."

"We can change that with time."

"I hope so. It won't help much to argue in court that I've got a wife to take care of my children, if my children hate her guts."

"We have a more immediate problem," Cherry said.

"What's that?"

"Zach Whitelaw."

"What about him?"

"He's going to kill you on sight."

Billy gave a relieved laugh. "Is that all? I thought it was something serious."

"Don't joke," Cherry said. "This is serious. Three years ago a boy tried to force himself on Jewel at a Fourth of July picnic. I'll never forget the look in Zach's eyes when Jewel stood crying in his arms, her face bruised and her dress torn. He took a horsewhip to the boy and nearly flayed him alive. Both families kept it quiet, but you know how that sort of thing gets around. None of us girls has ever had any problems with boys since then.

"That's why it surprised me when Ray... If Ray hadn't been drunk, he would never have done what he did."

"And we wouldn't be where we are today," Billy said. "I won't let any man whip me, Cherry. If your father tries—"

"I'm only telling you all this so you'll understand why I have to go home and explain all of this to him by myself. Once he understands I was willing and—"

Billy shook his head. "We go together, or you don't go at all."

"Zach's going to be furious with me."

"All the more reason for us to go together. You may have been his daughter yesterday, but you're my wife today. No man is going to threaten my wife. Not even her father."

Cherry stared wide-eyed at Billy. She supposed she should have told him that no matter how angry Zach got with her, he would never raise a hand to her. In the past she had been sent to her room without supper, or been forced to spend a day alone thinking about the wisdom of a course of action. But the Whitelaws had always used reason, rather than force, to teach their children right from wrong.

Billy wouldn't have to defend her, but she reveled in the thought that he was willing to do so. Of more concern to her was the possibility that the two men might provoke one another to violence. She already knew that Billy liked to fight. Zach would be more than willing to give him one.

"I'll let you come with me on one condition," she said.

"What's that?"

"We bring the girls with us."

Billy frowned. "What purpose would that serve?"

"Zach won't be able to fight with you—or yell at me—if he's busy meeting his new grandchildren."

"Raejean and Annie don't even like you. What makes you think they'll take to your father?"

"Trust me. Zach Whitelaw could sell snow in Alaska. He'll have Raejean and Annie eating out of his hand in no time. Besides, we have no choice but to take them with us. Mrs. Motherwell is gone.''

''I forgot about that,'' Billy said as he headed toward the door that led upstairs. ''Damn. All right. Let me go get them. We might as well get this meeting over with.''

''Billy,'' Cherry called after him. When he stopped and turned to her, she said, ''We can still call the whole thing off.''

He walked the few steps back to her and lifted her chin with his finger. ''Buck up, kid. You're doing great.''

Cherry felt tears prickle her eyes and blinked to keep them from forming.

Billy leaned down and kissed her mouth. His touch was gentle, intended to comfort. ''I'm sorry, Cherry. I shouldn't have left you here alone and driven away. It's not easy to admit it, but I was scared.''

Cherry searched his eyes. If he had once been afraid, the fear was gone now. If he had regrets, he wasn't letting her see them. She wished she knew him better as a person. Could she rely on him? Would he be there for her when the going got rough?

When he pulled her into his arms and hugged her, she felt safe and secure. She knew that was an illusion. Her father had made her feel safe, too. But they had been torn from each other. It was better not to try and make more of this relationship than it was.

Before she could edge herself away from Billy, the screen door was flung open. Billy threw her aside to confront whatever danger threatened them.

Zach Whitelaw stood in the doorway.

Five

"**D**addy, don't!" Cherry cried as Zach took a step toward Billy, his hands tightened into angry knots.

Zach froze, his eyes wide with shock.

It took Cherry a second to realize she had called him "Daddy" instead of "Zach," something she had never done before. She felt confused, unsure why she had blurted it out like that, especially now, when she wasn't going to be his daughter anymore, but someone else's wife.

"Please don't fight," she said.

"Stay out of this, Cherry," Billy said, his hands curling into fists as menacing as Zach's.

"How did you get here so quickly?" Cherry said to her father. "I just got off the phone with Jewel."

"The police called me when they picked up Billy. A phony marriage license isn't going to save you from me," he snarled at Billy.

"We really are married," Cherry said, taking a step to put herself between the two men. Temporarily, it kept them from throwing punches.

Zach snorted. "In a Las Vegas ceremony? That's no kind of wedding."

"It's legal," Billy said coldly.

There was nothing Zach could say to counter that except, "Come home, Cherry. I know the situation last night must have upset you, but Rebecca and I want you to know we're on your side. We believe there must be some reasonable explanation for what happened. We can fix this problem."

"It's too late for that. Billy and I are married. I'm staying with him."

Zach glared at Billy. "You should be ashamed of yourself, taking advantage of a vulnerable child to—"

"She's no child," Billy said quietly. "She's a woman. And my wife." His hands slid around Cherry's waist from behind, and he pulled her back against the length of his body.

Cherry saw the inference Zach drew from Billy's words and actions that the two of them had done what husbands and wives do on their wedding night.

By the time her father's gaze skipped to her face, she bore a flush high on her cheekbones that seemed to confirm what he was thinking. There was no way she was going to admit the truth.

She saw the wounded look in Zach's eyes before he hid it behind lowered lids.

"I didn't meant to hurt you or Rebecca," she forced past the lump in her throat.

"Why, Cherry?" he asked. "Why couldn't you trust us to be on your side? I thought..."

They were good parents. They had done everything they could to make her feel loved and appreciated, safe and secure. But they expected her to believe parents could protect their children from the evils of the world. She knew from experience that simply wasn't true. She could never trust them completely. She would never trust anybody that much again.

"I'm sorry, Zach." She saw his gaze flicker at her reversion to the less familiar, less personal title. "Please tell Rebecca—"

Zach cut her off. "You explain this to your mother. I couldn't find the words." He turned and left as abruptly as he had come.

Cherry felt her nose burning, felt the tears threaten and fought them back. She had chosen to travel this road. She had no one to blame but herself for her predicament. Crying over spilled milk wasn't going to accomplish anything.

"Thanks for sticking by me," Billy said against her ear.

"I'm your wife."

"Sometimes that doesn't mean much when parents enter the picture," Billy said bitterly.

Cherry turned in his embrace and put her arms around him to hug him, laying her cheek against his shoulder. "I'll try to be a good wife, Billy." She raised her face to his, only to find herself unexpectedly kissed.

There was as much desperation as there was hunger in Billy's kiss. Something inside Cherry responded to both emotions, and she found herself kissing Billy back.

"Hey! What are you doing to my dad?"

Cherry pulled free of Billy's grasp and turned to the urchin who had spoken. Behind her stood the other twin, her face less belligerent, more perplexed.

"Uh..." Cherry began. She had no idea where to go from there. She expected Billy to make some sort of explanation, but he gave her a helpless one-shouldered shrug. Cherry turned back to the twins and said to the one who had spoken, "Your dad and I were kissing, Raejean. That's what married people do."

"I'm Annie," Raejean said.

"I'm Raejean," Annie dutifully added.

"Hey, you two," Billy said. "What's the big idea trying to fool Cherry?"

Raejean's chin jutted. "I don't know why you're so mad, Daddy. She isn't fooled at all." She turned to Cherry, her brow furrowed. "How do you do that, anyway? No one but Mommy and Daddy has ever been able to tell us apart."

Cherry said, "There's nothing magic about it. You're as different from your sister as night from day."

"We're twins," Raejean protested. "We're *exactly* alike."

"You look alike on the outside," Cherry conceded, "but inside here—" Cherry touched her head. "And here—" She touched her heart. "You're very different."

"I'm glad you can tell us apart," Annie said. "I don't like fooling people."

"I don't care if you can tell us apart," Raejean said. "I'm not going to like you."

"Isn't it a little soon to make up your mind about that?" Cherry asked. "You hardly know me."

"I know you want to be my mother. I don't want another mother. My mother's in heaven!" Raejean turned and headed for the stairs. She hadn't gone very far before she realized Annie hadn't automatically followed her. She turned and said, "Come on, Annie."

Annie hesitated briefly before she turned and followed her sister.

Cherry whirled on Billy the instant they were gone. "I can't do this all by myself, Billy. You're going to have to help."

"You can't blame them for being confused, Cherry. After all, the only woman they've ever seen me kissing is their mother."

"Then maybe we shouldn't let the girls see us kissing. Maybe you should keep your distance when they're around."

Billy thought about it for a moment, then shook his head. "I don't want to do that for two reasons. Penelope would be sure to notice if we never touched each other. It would be a dead giveaway that there's something fishy about our marriage."

"And the second reason?"

"I don't want my daughters to see me ignoring the woman they believe is my wife. It would give them the wrong impression of what marriage is all about."

"I see." What she saw was that Billy had all sorts of reasons for kissing and hugging her that had nothing whatsoever to do with actually loving her. But loving hadn't been a part of their bargain. She had to remind herself of the rules of this game. *Help each other out. Don't get involved. Don't start to care.* That way lay heartache.

"All right, Billy," Cherry said. "I'll play along with you where the kissing and touching is concerned. So long as we both know it's only an act, I suppose neither of us can be hurt. Now that we have that settled, I believe you need to get to town for those supplies, and I'd better get some lunch started."

Cherry turned her back on Billy, but she hadn't taken two steps toward the sink before his arms slid around her from behind again, circling her waist. Her treacherous body melted against him. She forced herself to stiffen in his embrace. "Don't, Billy," she said in a quiet voice.

"You're my wife, Cherry."

"In name only," Cherry reminded him. "We can pretend for everybody else, but I think it's best if we're honest with each other. We aren't in love, Billy. We never will be."

Billy's hands dropped away, but he didn't move. She felt the heat of his body along the entire length of her back. Her eyes slid closed, and she held herself rigid to keep from leaning back into his fiery warmth.

"If we're being honest," Billy said in a husky voice, "I think you should know I'm more than a little attracted to you, Cherry. I have been since the moment I first laid eyes on you." Billy took her by the shoulders and turned her to face him. "That's the truth."

She lifted her eyes to meet his. "That's lust, Billy. Not love."

His dark eyes narrowed, and his hands dropped away from her shoulders. "There's nothing wrong with desiring your wife in bed."

"I'm not your wi—"

"Dammit, Cherry!"

When Billy took a step back and shoved his hands into his jeans pockets, Cherry had the distinct impression he did it to keep himself from reaching for her again.

"You *are* my wife," he said through gritted teeth. "Not forever. Not even for very long. But we most definitely are married. I suggest you start thinking that way!"

Before she could contradict him, he was gone, the screen door slamming behind him.

Billy couldn't remember a time when he had been more frustrated. Even when he had been arguing with Laura about whether or not she should try to get pregnant again when the doctor had advised her against it, he hadn't felt so much like he was butting his head against a stone wall. Deep down, he knew Cherry was right. It would be better for both of them if he kept his distance from her.

He had made up his mind to try.

Of course, that was before he stepped into Cherry's bedroom the morning after their wedding. He had expected her to be up and dressed, since he had helped her set the alarm for 5:30 a.m. the previous evening. Apparently, she had turned it off.

He found her sleeping beneath tousled sheets, one long, exquisite leg exposed all the way to her hip, one rosy nipple peeking at him, her lips slightly parted, her silky red curls spread across the pillow, waiting for a lover's hands to gather them up.

He cleared his throat noisily, hoping that would be enough to wake her. All she did was roll over, rearranging the sheet, exposing an entire milky white breast.

He swallowed hard and averted his eyes. He sat down beside her, thinking maybe the dip in the mattress would make her aware of his presence.

She slept on.

His gaze returned to rest on her face. Close as he was, he could see the dark shadows under her eyes. She must not have slept very well. He could understand that. He hadn't slept too well himself. He had resorted to a desperate act—marriage—to solve one problem and had created a host of others in the process. Not the least of which was the fact he wanted to have carnal knowledge of his new wife.

He debated whether he ought to kiss her awake. But he wasn't Prince Charming. And Sleeping Beauty had never had such a freckled face. Nevertheless, his body responded to the mere thought of pressing his lips against hers, of tasting the hot, sweet wetness of her mouth.

Billy swore viciously.

And Cherry woke with a start.

It took her a second to realize how exposed she was, and she grabbed at the sheet as she sat up and drew her knees to her chest. Her blue eyes were wide and wary. "What are you doing in here?"

"I came to wake you up. You overslept."

She glanced at the clock, then dropped her forehead to her knees and groaned. "I must have turned off the alarm."

"I figured as much when you didn't show up in the kitchen. I've already had my breakfast. I left some coffee perking for you. The kids'll be up in a little while. You probably have time for a quick shower."

Thinking about her naked in the shower had about the same effect as contemplating kissing her. Billy needed to leave, but he was too aware of what Cherry would see if he stood right now. So he went right on sitting where he was.

Unfortunately, she now had the sheet flattened against herself, and he could see the darker outline of her nipples beneath the soft cotton. He found that every bit as erotic as seeing her naked.

"Hell," Billy muttered, shifting uncomfortably on the edge of the bed.

"What's the matter?"

Billy's lip curled wryly. "I'm not used to looking at a woman in bed without being able to touch."

"Oh." She clutched the sheet tighter, exposing the fact that her nipples had become hard nubs.

Billy bolted to his feet and saw her gaze lock on the bulge beneath his zipper. He froze where he was, his body aching, his mouth dry.

He watched her until she lifted her eyes to his face. Her pupils were enormous, her lips full, as though he had been kissing her. She was aroused, and he hadn't even touched her.

"Tell me to go, Cherry." He wanted to consume her in a hurry, like ice cream on a hot day. He wanted to take his time and sip at her slow and easy, like a cool mint julep on a lazy summer afternoon.

She licked her lips, and he felt his body harden like stone.

"The girls will be up soon," Cherry reminded him. "I need to get dressed."

Heaven help him, he had forgotten all about his daughters. He shoved a distracted hand through his hair and huffed out a breath of air. "I'll be working on the range today. If you need anything..."

Cherry smiled. "Don't worry about us, Billy. We'll manage fine."

"All right. So long."

He was almost out the door when she called him back.

"Billy?"

He turned and found her standing beside the bed with the sheet draped around her in a way that revealed as much as it covered. "What?" he asked, his voice hoarse from the sudden rush of desire he felt.

"You didn't kiss me goodbye."

He shook his head. "I don't think that would be a good idea, Cherry."

Before he realized what she had in mind, she closed the few steps between them and lifted her face to him. "I thought a lot about our situation last night, when I couldn't sleep," she said earnestly. "And I realized that if we're going to convince Mrs. Trask that this is a real marriage, we're going to have to act as much like a happily married couple as possible.

"Zach always gives Rebecca a kiss goodbye in the morning." She gave him a winsome smile. "So, pucker up, Mr. Stonecreek, and give me a kiss."

She didn't give him much of a choice. She raised herself on tiptoe and leaned forward and pressed her lips against his.

Billy gathered her in his arms and pulled her close as his mouth opened over hers, taking what he had denied himself only moments before. His hands slid down her naked back, shoving the sheet out of his way. Then he held her buttocks tight against his arousal with one hand while the other caught her nape and slid up to grasp a handful of her hair.

He took his time kissing her, his tongue thrusting hard and deep, and then slowing for several soft, probing forays, seeking the honey within. She made a moaning sound deep in her throat, and he gave an answering growl of passion.

When he let her go at last, she gave him a dazed look through half-closed lids, then grabbed at the sheet that had slid down to her waist and pulled it back up to cover herself. He grinned and said, "That was a good idea. I think we'll keep it up."

It took all the willpower he had to turn and walk out the bedroom door.

Cherry watched Billy go this time without calling him back. She was still quivering from his kiss. She forced her wobbly legs to take one step, and then another, as she headed for the bentwood rocker where she had thrown her robe. She slipped it on and let the sheet drop to the floor.

She was tying her terry-cloth robe closed when she heard a knock on the door. She hurried to open it and found Billy standing there with his hat on, his hip cocked, and his thumbs in his front pockets.

"Did you forget something?" she asked.

Not a thing, Billy realized. He remembered exactly how she had looked in bed. *And you look as delicious in that robe as you did in bed.* He couldn't very well tell her he had come back just to look at her again. So he said, "I forgot to say good morning." He smiled and tipped his hat. "Mornin', ma'am."

Cherry laughed.

And then, because he was looking for an excuse to spend more time with her, he said, "I wondered if you'd like to join me for a cup of coffee before I leave."

"I should get dressed," Cherry said, tightening the belt on her robe. "The girls will be up soon."

"You're right about that." Billy searched for something else to say, because otherwise he would have no excuse to linger.

"By the way, I never got around to telling you, but you'll need to go grocery shopping today. The ranch has an account at the store in town. I think Harvey Mills already knows we're married—I doubt there's anyone in the county who doesn't know by now—but just in case, I'll give him a call and tell him to put your name on the account. Feel free to get anything you think we'll need."

It was more than Cherry had heard Billy say at one time since she had met him at the pond. But the words had nothing to do with what he was saying with his eyes. His eyes were eating her alive. Her heart was pumping hard. Her breasts felt full. Her mouth felt dry.

She cleared her throat and said, "Shopping. Got it. Anything else?"

"Not unless you'd like that cup of coffee."

Cherry slowly shook her head. She had to send him away or she was going to invite him into her room. "I need to shower and dress before the girls wake up. Have a nice day, Billy."

"Yeah. I'll do that."

When he didn't leave, she raised a brow and said, "Is there something else, Billy?"

"If you want, I can go with you later today to see your family... to explain things."

Cherry felt a sense of relief. "Thanks, Billy. I'd like that."

"Well. I guess I'd better get started."

It took him another moment or two before he moved away from the door. She watched his sexy, loose-limbed amble until he was gone from sight, then scurried up the stairs to the shower.

However, when she reached the bathroom, it was locked. She would have to wait her turn. She leaned against the wall, a towel over her arm, one bare foot perched atop the other and waited. And waited. The door never opened.

She leaned her ear against the door, but there was no sound coming from inside. She knocked and said, "Is someone in there?"

No answer.

"Raejean? Annie?"

Nothing.

She walked down the hall to the girls' bedroom. Their unmade twin beds were empty. She checked the other doors along the hall and found an office and Billy's bedroom, but no sign of the children.

"Raejean!" she called loudly. "Annie! If you're hiding somewhere up here, I want you to come out right now!"

Nothing.

She crossed back to the bathroom door and listened intently. She thought she heard whispers. She banged on the door. "I know you two are in there. I want you to come out right now."

Nothing.

She grabbed the doorknob and yanked on it, then slammed her shoulder against the door as though to break it open. "Open up!"

Nothing.

Cherry leaned back against the wall and sighed heavily. She hadn't counted on this sort of misbehavior when she had nobly volunteered to rescue Billy's daughters from their grandmother's clutches. Right now, Mrs. Trask was more than welcome to the two of them!

Cherry smiled. Actually, she had pulled the same trick on one of her foster parents. She had spent almost two days in the bathroom before hunger finally forced her out. Which gave her an idea.

"All right, fine, stay in there. But you're going to get awfully hungry before the day is out. I'm going downstairs and make myself some blueberry pancakes with whipped cream on top and scrambled eggs and sausage and wash it all down with some hot chocolate with marshmallows."

Loud, agitated whispers.

The bathroom door opened and one of the twins stuck her head out. "Whipped cream on pancakes?"

Cherry nodded.

An identical face appeared and asked, "Big marshmallows? Or little ones?"

"Which do you prefer?"

"Little ones. Mrs. Motherwell only bought the big ones."

"Then we'll cut them into little pieces," Cherry suggested.

"All right." Annie shot out of the bathroom before Raejean could stop her and took Cherry by the hand. "Let's go."

Cherry waited to see what Raejean would do. The twin obviously wasn't happy to see rebellion in the ranks. She seemed unsure whether to stay where she was or abandon the fort. Her stomach growled and settled the matter. Raejean left the bathroom and headed down the hall toward the stairs, ignoring the hand Cherry held out to her.

Cherry realized as she followed Raejean down the stairs, Annie chattering excitedly beside her, that she might have won this battle, but the war had just begun.

Six

Breakfast was a huge success. Cherry sat at the kitchen table giving herself a pat on the back for having pleased both girls so well. Two plates had been licked clean. Annie must have eaten almost as many additional marshmallows as the two of them had cut up together for her hot chocolate. Raejean had devoured the entire batch of whipped cream. The kitchen was a mess, but Cherry would have time to clean it once the twins were at school.

"Uh-oh," Annie said.

"Daddy's going to be *really* mad," Raejean said.

Cherry followed the direction of the girls' gazes out the kitchen window and saw the school bus at the end of the lane. It paused momentarily, honked, and when no one appeared, continued on its way.

"Oh, no!" Cherry raced to the back door, yanked it open and shouted to the bus driver. "Wait!"

He didn't hear her, which was just as well, because when she turned back to the kitchen she realized the girls weren't dressed and their hair wasn't combed.

Billy hadn't asked much of her—only that she feed his children breakfast and get them to school and be there when they got home in the afternoon. She couldn't even manage that.

She looked at the clock. Seven-thirty in the morning and she was already a failure as a stepmother. Before despair could take hold, it dawned on her that elementary school surely couldn't start this early. Maybe she could still get the girls there on time.

"When do classes start?" she asked Raejean.

"Eight o'clock sharp," Raejean answered. "Mrs. Winslow gets *really* mad if we're late."

"You still have time to get there if we move like lightning," Cherry said.

She hurried the girls upstairs, but the more urgency she felt, the slower they both seemed to move. She ended up accidentally yanking Annie's hair as she shoved the hairbrush through a knot.

"Ouch!" Annie cried. "That hurt."

Cherry was instantly contrite. She had too much experience of her own with substitute parents who were in too much of a hurry to be gentle with her. She went down on one knee in the bathroom beside Annie and said, "I'm sorry, Annie. I should have been more careful. I guess I'm worried that I won't get you to school on time."

"Yeah. And Daddy will be *really* mad," Raejean reminded her through a mouthful of toothpaste.

"Spit and rinse," Cherry ordered Raejean as she finished putting Annie's hair into pigtails. "I'll get to you next."

For a moment Raejean seemed to consider putting up a fight, but she stood still while Cherry pulled the brush through her tangled hair.

"My mom always put ribbons in our hair," Raejean said.

Cherry heard the wistful longing in the complaint, but there wasn't time to fulfill any wishes this morning. "Tonight we'll see what we can find and have them ready for tomorrow morning," she promised.

It wasn't until she had dressed herself and was ushering the girls out the back door that she realized she had no idea what they were going to use for transportation. There had to be some vehicle available, because Billy had suggested she go shopping during the day. But the only thing on four wheels she saw was a rusted-out pickup near the barn.

A set of hooks inside the back door held a key attached to a rabbit's foot. She grabbed the key, shoved the girls out the door, and prayed the truck had an automatic transmission.

It didn't.

"Don't you know how to drive?" Annie asked, concern etched in her young brow.

"I can drive. I have the license to prove it."

"Then why aren't we moving?" Annie asked.

Cherry stared helplessly at the stick shift on the floor of the pickup. "I'm not sure how to get this thing into gear." She tried moving the stick, and it made an ominous grinding sound.

"If you break Daddy's truck, he's going to be *really* mad," Raejean said.

Cherry was getting the picture. If she didn't figure out something soon, she was going to be dealing with a seriously annoyed teacher when she got the girls to school and a fierce, wild-eyed beast of a man when Billy got home.

She crossed her arms on the steering wheel and leaned her head down to think. She could call her sister Jewel to come rescue her, but that was so mortifying a prospect she immediately rejected it. She felt a small hand tapping her shoulder.

"I can show you how to do it," Annie volunteered.

Cherry lifted her head and stared suspiciously at the six-year-old. "You know how to drive a stick shift?"

"Sure," Annie said. "Daddy lets us do it all the time."

Since there wasn't anyone else to show her how, Cherry said, "All right. Go ahead and show me what to do."

"Put your foot on that pedal down there first," Annie said. "Turn the key, and then move this thing here."

Cherry pushed down the clutch, turned on the ignition, and reached for the black gearshift knob. To her amazement the gearshift moved easily without making a sound. However, she ended up in third gear, didn't give the truck enough gas, and let the clutch go too fast. The pickup stalled.

"You have to follow the numbers," Raejean chided, pointing to the black gearshift knob. "See? One, two, three, four, and R."

"R isn't a number," Cherry pointed out.

"R is for reverse," Annie piped up.

Maybe Billy did let them drive, Cherry thought. At least they knew more about a stick shift than she did. "All right. Here goes."

It was touch and go at first, but she managed to get the truck into second gear, and they chugged down the lane headed for the highway. She stalled a couple of times and ground the gears more than once before she got the hang of it. But she felt proud of herself when she finally pulled into the school parking lot and killed the engine.

"We made it," she said, glancing at her wristwatch. "With five minutes to spare."

"You forgot our lunches," Raejean said.

"What lunches?"

"Mrs. Motherwell always made us a sack lunch. We're going to starve," Annie said.

"Daddy's going to be *really* mad," Raejean said.

"Maybe you could buy your lunches today," Cherry suggested.

"I guess we could," Raejean conceded.

Annie and Raejean held out their hands for money.

Cherry realized she hadn't brought her purse with her. She checked both her jeans pockets and came up empty. "Look, I'll go home and make lunches for you and bring them back to school. How would that be?"

"Okay, I guess," Raejean said.

"I don't feel so good," Annie said, her hand on her stomach.

"Probably all the excitement this morning," Cherry said sympathetically. "You'll feel better once you're settled in class. Have a nice day, Raejean. Enjoy yourself, Annie."

She watched the two girls make their way inside, Raejean skipping and Annie holding on to her stomach.

To be honest, her own stomach was churning. It had been a hectic morning. And it wasn't over yet. She had to get home, make lunches and get back, then get the kitchen and the house cleaned up before the girls got home in the afternoon.

It was a lot of responsibility for someone whose biggest problem before today was whether she could figure out her calculus homework or get the formulas right in chemistry class. The entire responsibility for the house and two lively children now rested on her shoulders. It was an awesome burden.

She should have thought of that sooner. Now that she had made the commitment, she was determined to see it through. There were bound to be a few glitches at first. The important thing was to keep on trying until she succeeded.

Of course, she wasn't going anywhere until she figured out how to get the pickup into reverse. No matter how many times she put the gearshift where she thought R ought to be, she couldn't get the truck to back up. When the final tardy bell rang, she was still sitting there.

She was going to have to call Jewel after all.

"Hey, Cherry, what's the matter?"

Cherry looked up into the sapphire blue eyes of her eleven-year-old brother, Colt. A black curl had slipped from his ponytail and curled around his ear. He was wearing tight jeans instead of the frumpy ones currently in style, and a white T-shirt and cowboy boots reminiscent of James Dean. Colt truly was the rebel in the family. But he somehow convinced everybody that doing things his way was their idea.

Cherry glanced at the empty schoolyard and said, "You're late, Colt."

He grinned. "Yeah. Looks that way."

"You don't seem too concerned about it. Zach will be—" Cherry stopped herself when she realized she was about to echo Raejean and say "*really* mad."

"Dad knows I'm late," Colt said. "Things were a little crazy this morning because of you disappearing and all. You really did it this time, Cherry. Mom went ballistic when she heard what you did, and Dad hasn't come down off the ceiling since he got back from the Stonecreek Ranch. Are you really married to Billy Stonecreek?"

"Uh-huh."

"Neat. He really knows how to use his fists to defend himself." Colt shrugged his book bag off and did some shadow boxing. He was tall for his age, his body lean, his movements graceful. "Billy's been in three fights this year," he said. "Do you think he'd show me a few punches?"

"Absolutely not! And where did you find out all this information about Billy?" Cherry asked.

"I heard Mom and Dad talking. They're worried that Billy's a bad influence on you. They said he's gonna undo all the hard work they've done, and you're gonna end up back in trouble again."

Cherry felt her face heating. Not that she didn't appreciate what Zach and Rebecca had done for her. But she had come a long way since the days when she had habitually cut school and been ready to fight the world.

"You'd better get inside," she told Colt.

"It's all right. Mom called and told them I'd be late," Colt replied. "What are you doing here?"

"I drove Raejean and Annie Stonecreek to school."

"Why didn't they take the bus?"

"They missed the bus."

Colt grinned. "Overslept, huh? You never were very good at getting up in the morning."

"Not that it's any of your business, but I didn't oversleep. I merely lost track of the time."

"Same difference," Colt said. "So why aren't you headed back home?"

"I can't figure out how to get this damn truck into reverse."

Colt laughed. "It's easy. Press the stick down and over."

"Press down? You have to press *down* on the stick before you move it?"

"Sure."

Cherry tried it, gave the truck a little gas, and felt it move backward. "Good grief," she muttered. "Thanks, Colt. I owe you one."

"Will you ask Billy if he'll show me a few punches?"

"I'll think about it," she replied as she backed out of the parking lot. "Tell Rebecca I'll come see her tonight," she called out the window as she drove away.

It was the coward's way out to have Colt relay her message. She should have called Rebecca and told her she was coming. But she didn't want to be forced into explaining things to her mother over the phone, and she knew Rebecca must be anxious for some sort of explanation for what she had done. The truth was, she needed the rest of the day to think of one.

By the time she made it back to the ranch she was a pro at shifting gears. She parked the truck behind the house, stepped inside the kitchen, and realized it looked like a tornado had been through. What if Billy came back home for some reason and saw it looking like this?

But she didn't want to stop and clean it right now and take a chance on being late with the girls' lunches. The mess was even worse by the time she finished making sandwiches. She vowed to clean up the kitchen as soon as she returned. She was out the door half an hour later, sack lunches in hand.

When she arrived at the principal's office, Cherry was surprised to be told that Annie still wasn't feeling well. Her teacher had asked the office to call the house and have someone come and pick her up.

"I was concerned when I couldn't reach anyone at the ranch," the principal said, "so I called Mrs. Trask."

"Oh, no," Cherry groaned. "Call her back, please, and tell her it isn't necessary to come. I'll take Annie home."

"I'll try," the principal said. "But she's probably already on her way."

Cherry's only thought was to get Annie and leave as quickly as possible.

"I'm Cherry Whitelaw, Mrs. Winslow," she said when she arrived at Annie's classroom. Cherry flushed. "Except it's Stonecreek now. My name, I mean. I'm here for Annie."

"She's lying on a cot at the back of the room, Mrs. Stonecreek. Raejean insisted on sitting with her."

It felt strange to be called by her married name. Only she really was Mrs. Stonecreek, and responsible for the twins' welfare. She sat on a chair beside the cot and brushed the bangs away from Annie's forehead. "How are you, sweetheart?"

Annie moaned. "My stomach hurts."

"She ate too many marshmallows," Raejean said from her perch beside her sister.

"Marshmallows?" Mrs. Winslow asked.

"Annie had a few marshmallows with her hot chocolate this morning," Cherry said.

"How many is a few?" Mrs. Winslow asked.

Cherry hadn't counted. "Too many, I guess. Can you walk, Annie? Or do I need to carry you?"

Annie sat up, holding her stomach. "I don't feel so good."

Cherry picked her up in her arms.

"Where are you taking her?" Raejean demanded.

"Home," Cherry said.

"I'm going, too," Raejean said.

"There's no reason for you to miss a day of school," Cherry said reasonably. "I'll take good care of Annie."

"How do I know that?" Raejean demanded. "You're practically a stranger!"

"Raejean," Mrs. Winslow said. "Mrs. Stonecreek is right. There's no reason for you to leave."

"I'm going with Annie," Raejean said to Mrs. Winslow, her face flushed. "I'm not staying here alone."

"You won't be alone," Mrs. Winslow soothed. "You'll—"

"I'm going with Annie!" Raejean cried.

"Raejean—" Cherry began.

"I'm going with Annie!" she screeched hysterically.

Cherry knew the dangers of giving in to a tantrum. But in her mind's eye she saw Mrs. Trask arriving to find a scene like this and knew she was over a barrel. "All right, Raejean, you can come. I'm sorry for the trouble, Mrs. Winslow."

She turned and headed for the door with Annie in her arms and Raejean a half step behind her. She was almost out the door when Mrs. Trask showed up.

"What's the matter with my granddaughter? What have you done to her?" she demanded.

"Annie is fine, Mrs. Trask." Cherry kept moving down the hall toward the front door of the school, still hoping to escape without a major confrontation.

"Annie's sick because she ate too many marshmallows," Raejean volunteered.

"Marshmallows?" Mrs. Trask said as though what she was really saying was "Poison?"

"Annie will be fine, Mrs. Trask."

"I was afraid of something like this. You're not responsible enough to be left in charge of two little girls."

Cherry didn't want to admit Mrs. Trask might be right. She had misjudged the situation this morning, but that didn't mean she couldn't do better. She would learn. After all, nobody had practice being a parent before they actually became one.

"Thank you for coming, Mrs. Trask, but as you can see, I have the situation well in hand."

"I'm coming home with you," Mrs. Trask said.

"I don't believe that's necessary," Cherry countered.

"I—"

"What's going on here?"

Cherry stopped in her tracks.

It was Billy. He didn't look *really* mad, as Raejean had promised. He looked frantic, his brow furrowed, his sweat-stained work shirt pulled out of his jeans and hanging open, revealing a hairy chest covered with a damp sheen of sweat. He was still wearing his buckskin work gloves, but he was missing his hat. He had obviously shoved an agitated hand through his dark hair more than once, leaving it awry. He looked virile and strong . . . and very worried.

"I stopped by the house for some tools and found you gone and a message on the answering machine that Annie wasn't feeling well. Is she all right?"

"I'm sick, Daddy," Annie cried.

For a moment Cherry thought Billy would take Annie from her. Instead he asked, "Do you need any help with her?"

"I can manage if you'll get the door to the pickup."

"I knew something like this would happen," Mrs. Trask said to Billy as they all headed outside to the rusted pickup.

"Something like what, Penelope?" Billy said.

"Something awful."

"Kids get stomachaches, Penelope," Billy said.

"Not if parents are careful and watch what they eat."

"Look, Penelope, I appreciate you coming, but Cherry and I can handle things now."

"How can you trust that woman—"

Billy turned on his former mother-in-law, and for the first time Cherry saw the anger Raejean had threatened. "*That woman* is my wife. And I have the utmost trust in her to take the very best care possible of Raejean and Annie."

"Well, I don't."

"You don't have anything to say about it, Penelope."

"We'll see about that! The day is coming—"

Billy cut her off again. "You'll have your day in court, Penelope. Until then, I can manage my family just fine without any help from you."

Cherry was impressed by Billy's support of her. She had done nothing to deserve his trust, and yet he had given it to her. She wanted very much to prove his faith in her was well-founded. She was simply going to have to try a little harder to be responsible.

"I'll follow you back to the house," Billy said to her as he buckled Raejean into her seat belt. "Maybe we can figure out what made Annie sick."

"She ate too many marshmallows," Raejean volunteered.

"What the hell was she doing eating marshmallows at breakfast?" Billy demanded of Cherry.

"I gave them to her," Cherry confessed. "With her hot chocolate. I guess I gave her a few too many."

Billy opened his mouth and snapped it shut on whatever criticism was caught in his throat. "We'll discuss this when we get home." He turned and marched to the other truck, a pickup in much better shape than the one she was driving.

The ride home was silent except for an occasional moan from Annie. When they arrived home, Billy carried Annie inside with Raejean trailing behind him. Billy breezed through the chaos in the kitchen without a pause and headed for the stairs. Cherry followed them, feeling as unwelcome as red ants at a picnic.

She stood at the bedroom door watching as Billy tucked Annie into bed and settled Raejean at a small desk with a coloring book and some crayons. She was amazed at his patience with his daughters. Amazed at his calm, quiet voice as he talked to them. The longer she watched, the worse she felt.

Billy had needed someone to help him out. All she had done was cause more trouble. Maybe he would want out of the marriage now. Maybe that's what he wanted to discuss with her.

When he rose at last and came toward her, he indicated with a nod that she should precede him down the stairs. Cherry felt the tension mounting as she headed into the kitchen, where the peanut butter jar stood open and blobs of jelly lay smeared on the counter. A pan bearing the scraped remnants of scrambled eggs sat in the sink, along with one lined with scalded milk.

She turned to face Billy. "I can explain everything," she said.

That was when he started laughing.

Seven

"What's so funny?" Cherry demanded.

"Annie eating all those marshmallows. She probably begged you for more."

"How did you know?"

"Laura and I let the twins eat too much ice cream the first time they tried it. It's hard to deny them anything when you see how much they're enjoying it. You'll learn." His expression sobered as he added, "That's what parents have to do, Cherry. They have to set limits and stand by them, for the sake of the kids."

"I'll try to do better, Billy," she replied.

Rather than say more, he merely scooped her into his arms, gave her a hug and said, "I've got to get back to mending fence. See you at supper."

It wasn't until he was out the door and gone that she realized he hadn't said a word about the sorry state of the kitchen. Cherry took a look around. There was no way he hadn't noticed. She blessed him for not criticizing, and decided to reward him with a sparkling kitchen when he next saw it.

Of course, that was before she knew what the afternoon held in store.

Grocery shopping was out of the question because Annie was in bed sick, so she took some hamburger out of the freezer to defrost for meatloaf while she cleaned up the kitchen. When she went to check on the twins, she found Annie sound asleep.

Raejean was gone.

She searched the entire house, high and low, without finding her. "She couldn't have left the house. I would have seen her," Cherry muttered to herself.

Unless she went out the front door.

Cherry found the front door open a crack.

"Oh, no, Raejean."

She was afraid to leave Annie alone in the house while she searched, but she knew she had to find Raejean before Billy came home. It was one thing to let a child overeat; it was quite another to lose one entirely. She had no choice but to call for help.

"Jewel, can you come over here?"

"What's wrong, Cherry? Should I get Mom and Dad?"

"No! I'm sure I can handle this. Would you please just come over?"

When she was home from college, Jewel helped run Camp Littlehawk, a retreat that Rebecca had started years ago at Hawk's Pride for kids with cancer. Summer sessions hadn't yet begun, so Jewel was free to come and go as she pleased.

"I'll be there in thirty minutes," Jewel said. "Is that soon enough?"

"No. But I guess it'll have to do."

"It sounds serious, Cherry. Are you sure—"

"I'm sure I can handle it with your help, Jewel. Please hurry."

The next thirty minutes were the longest of Cherry's life. Billy had shown a tremendous amount of trust in her, and she had already let him down once. She had to find Raejean before anything happened to her.

"How can I help?" Jewel asked the instant she came through the kitchen door.

With that single question, Jewel proved what a gem of a sister she was and why she was Cherry's favorite sibling. Jewel gave a thousand percent to whatever she did and never asked for anything in return.

She walked with a slight limp, a result of the car wreck that had orphaned her, and her face bore faint, criss-crossing scars from the same accident. She had mud-brown eyes and dishwater-blond curls, and looked so ordinary you wouldn't see her in a crowd. But she had a heart so big it made her an extraordinary human being.

"I'm in way over my head, Jewel," Cherry confessed. "I thought taking care of two little girls was going to be a breeze. It isn't."

"What's the problem?" Jewel asked.

"Annie's upstairs in bed sick, and Raejean's missing. I need you to watch Annie while I hunt for Raejean."

"I'll be glad to do that. Are you sure you don't want some more help hunting down Raejean?"

"I'd rather try to find her myself first. With any luck, she's hiding somewhere close to the house."

Cherry looked in the barn, which was the most obvious place for the little girl to hide. It was dark and cool and smelled of hay and leather and manure. A search of the stalls turned up two geldings and a litter of kittens, but no little girl.

She climbed the ladder that led to the loft and gave it a quick look, but there was nothing but hay bales and feed sacks, so she climbed down again. As she turned to leave the barn, she heard a sound in the loft. Several pieces of straw wafted through the air and landed on the cement floor in front of her.

"I know you're up there, Raejean," she said. "Please come down. I've been very worried about you."

Footsteps sounded on the wooden floor above her before Raejean said, "You have not! I'm not coming down till my Daddy gets home."

Cherry climbed the ladder to the loft and followed the sounds of a sobbing child to the feed sacks in the corner. Raejean was huddled there, her knees wrapped up in her arms, her stubborn jaw outthrust as she glared at her new stepmother.

Cherry sat on the scattered straw across from Raejean. "I know what it feels like to lose your mother, Raejean. I know what it feels like to have a stranger try to boss you around. I'm sorry your mother died. I'm sorry she isn't here right now. I know I can never replace her. But your Daddy asked me to take care of you and Annie for him while he works every day. Won't you let me help him?"

Raejean's tear-drenched eyes lowered as she picked at a loose thread on the knee of her coveralls. "I miss my mommy. I want my nana."

Cherry's heart climbed to her throat. She could understand Raejean's need for the familiar. In the ordinary course of things, it would have been wonderful to have the girls' grandmother take care of them temporarily. But Mrs. Trask wanted to wrench them away from their father permanently. Cherry wasn't willing to worry Raejean with that possibility, but she wasn't going to encourage Raejean's desire to run to her grandmother for solace, either.

"I'm sure your daddy will take you to visit your grandmother soon. Right now we need to go back inside and check on Annie. I invited my sister, Jewel, to stay with her while I looked for you, but I think Annie needs us."

"She doesn't need you!" Raejean retorted.

"Maybe not. But she needs you. Will you come back inside with me?"

Cherry's heart sank when the little girl said nothing. What was she supposed to do now? She couldn't very well drag Raejean down the ladder. And while she could probably let her sit up here until Billy came home, it wasn't a particularly safe place for a six-year-old.

She put a comforting hand on Raejean's shoulder, but the child shrugged it off. "Please, Raejean? I need your help with Annie."

"Oh, all right," Raejean said. "But I'm coming inside for Annie. Not for you."

Her face remained sullen as she followed Cherry inside, and she glowered when she discovered that Annie was still asleep.

"Maybe while Annie's sleeping you could help me make supper," Cherry cajoled.

"I don't know how to cook," Raejean said. "Mrs. Motherwell wouldn't let us in the kitchen, and Nana has a lady to do all her cooking."

"Would you like to learn?"

Reluctantly Raejean nodded her head.

"Let's give it a try, shall we?"

"If the emergency is over, I've got some chores I need to do this afternoon," Jewel said.

"I'll walk you to your car," Cherry said. "I'll be back in a few minutes, Raejean. Then we can get started on supper."

"When will I see you again?" Jewel asked as they headed downstairs.

"I told Colt I was going to bring the girls and Billy to meet Zach and Rebecca this evening, but I think I'd better revise that plan. Will you tell Rebecca that Annie's not well, and that we'll come visit as soon as we can?"

"Why don't you call her yourself?" Jewel urged as Cherry walked her out to her car. "I know she wants to talk to you."

"I can't face her, Jewel. Not after the way I disappointed her again."

"You know Mom and Dad are proud of you."

"Most of the time."

"You're their daughter. They love you."

"I don't know why," Cherry said with a sigh.

Jewel shook her head. "There's no rhyme or reason to loving someone. You should know that by now." She gave Cherry a hug. "Take care, Mrs. Stonecreek."

"Please don't call me that, Jewel."

"Why not? You're married, aren't you?"

"Yes." *Temporarily.* "It feels strange, that's all. It's a marriage of convenience," she confessed. "Billy needed someone to take care of his girls, and I—I couldn't face Zach and Rebecca after what happened at the prom."

"I figured it might be something like that."

Cherry could tell Jewel was curious, but Jewel didn't ask questions. She merely smiled and gave Cherry another hug. "Call me if you need me, okay?"

As Jewel drove away, Cherry turned back to the house, to perhaps the biggest challenge of her life—being a mother to two little girls who didn't want one.

Billy entered the kitchen at dusk, after a long, discouraging day that had included a visit to a lawyer, to find utter chaos.

The open peanut butter and jelly jars were gone from the counter, replaced by catsup and a round container of oatmeal. Dirty dishes no longer sat in the sink; it was filled with potato peels. The kitchen smelled like something good was cooking in the oven. But instead of a table set for supper, he found three flour-dusted faces standing on a flour-dusted floor, laboring over a flour-dusted table.

"Hi, Daddy!" Raejean's face bore perhaps the biggest smile Billy had seen there since Laura's death. She held a rolling pin in her small hands and was mashing it across some dough spread on the table. "We're cooking."

"Hi, Daddy!" Annie's grin was equally large. She held up two flour-dusted hands, one of which held a hunk of half-eaten dough. "We're making an apple pie for you, because it's your favorite!"

Billy finally let his gaze come to rest on Cherry. She had been in his thoughts too often during the day. She had a panicked look on her face as she glanced around at the mess in the kitchen. She pointed to the dough in Annie's hand and said, "I only let her have this little bit. It's not enough to make her sick."

"I see," Billy said.

What Billy saw was Cherry reassuring him that she had learned her lesson. That she was willing to take responsibility for being the adult when she was barely one herself.

"We're running a little late," Cherry said, rubbing her hands across the front of her jeans and leaving them flour-dusted, as well. "After we got the meatloaf and mashed potatoes prepared, there was still time before we expected you back, so we decided to make a pie."

"I see."

What Billy saw was something he had never seen when Laura was alive, and likely never would have seen, even if she had lived. Laura had never learned to cook, and she didn't pretend to be any good at it or take any joy in it. The only apple pie she had ever made for him had come from a frozen food box. Culinary expertise hadn't been high on Billy's list of requirements for a wife, so he had never minded.

Now he realized what he had been missing. To see the three of them working together to make something especially for him touched a place deep inside of him. It fed a hunger for the sort of hearth and home that he imagined others experienced, but which had been lost to him since his parents' deaths. It was an added bonus to see Raejean and Annie so happy.

A different man might have seen only the mess and not the loving gesture that had been the source of it. Billy merely said, "Would you mind if I take a quick shower before I join you? I'm a little rank after a day on the range."

Cherry looked relieved. "That'll be fine. It'll give us time to finish up here."

He started for the hall but turned around before he got there and returned to the table. He saw the wariness in Cherry's eyes, the vulnerable look that said, "What have I done wrong now?"

He brushed a patch of flour from her cheek with his thumb before he lowered his mouth to touch hers. The shock was electric. When he could breathe again, he said, "Thanks, Cherry. Homemade apple pie will be a real treat."

"I helped," Raejean said.

"Me, too," Annie added.

Billy gave each of them a quick kiss on the nose. "I can tell," he said with a smile. "You two need a shower almost as bad as I do."

He made himself leave them and go shower, even though he was tempted to stay. He had to remind himself that Cherry was only there for a little while. Long enough to keep Penelope at bay. Long enough to make sure he kept custody of his kids.

By the time he got back downstairs, the pie was in the oven and the kitchen had undergone a partial transformation. The sink was stacked high with everything that had been on the table, but the floor was swept clear, and Cherry and his daughters no longer sported a liberal dusting of flour on their faces and clothes.

"I set the table," Raejean said proudly.

"It looks great," Billy said as he eyed the knife and fork on a folded paper napkin beside his plate.

"I picked the flowers," Annie said.

A collection of blue morning glories with tiny, half-inch stems floated in a bowl of water.

"They're beautiful," Billy said as he sat down and joined them at the kitchen table. "Your mother..." His throat closed suddenly. The swell of emotion surprised him. He had thought he had finished grieving. But the senseless tragedy of Laura's death was there with him again, as though it hadn't happened a full year in the past, but only yesterday.

The two girls looked at him expectantly, waiting for him to finish. He swallowed back the lump in his throat and managed to say, "Your mother would have loved to see them there."

"It was Cherry's idea," Annie volunteered. "She said they would be pretty."

"They are," Billy agreed softly. He let his gaze slip to Cherry for the first time since he had come to the table. "Morning glories were Laura's favorite flower," he said.

"I didn't know," she replied. "I can take them off the table, if you like."

"No. Leave them there. It's all right." He had to keep on living. He had to go on despite the fact Laura was no longer with him. He fought back the anger at Laura for leaving him alone to raise their two girls. It didn't help to feel angry. Better not to feel anything.

Only, that wasn't possible anymore. Not with Cherry living in the same house. Just looking at her made him feel way too much. He wanted her. And felt guilty because of it, even though he knew that was foolish. He was still alive. He still had needs. And she was his wife.

Temporarily. And only as a matter of convenience.

That didn't seem to matter to his body. It thrummed with excitement every time he looked at her. He wondered how her breasts would feel in his hands. He wondered whether she had freckles everywhere. He wanted to see her blue eyes darken with passion for him.

He was damned glad she couldn't read his mind.

After supper, the two little girls who had enjoyed making pie were less willing to clean up the results of their handiwork.

"Mrs. Motherwell always did the dishes by herself," Raejean protested.

"Yeah," Annie added.

"Maybe so, but she isn't here anymore," Cherry said. "Now everybody helps in the kitchen."

Raejean's eyes narrowed as though gauging whether she had to obey this dictum. She glanced at her father, still sitting at the table finishing up his second slice of pie, and asked, "Even Daddy?"

Billy had been listening to the byplay between Cherry and his daughters, a little surprised that she expected the twins to help. There was nothing wrong with them learning to do their share of the chores. Of course, he hadn't expected to be included. Dishes were women's work.

Now what, smart guy? Are you going to act like a male chauvinist pig? Or are you going to provide a good example to your children and pitch in to help?

Billy rose and carried his plate to the sink. "All of us have to do our part," he said. "Even me."

It was fun.

He had never done dishes as a family project, but there were definite advantages to doing the work as a team. Like having the girls tease him with the sprayer in the sink as they stood on a chair and rinsed off the dishes before Cherry loaded them in the dishwasher. And tickling Cherry, who turned out to be the most ticklish person he had ever known.

In the past, jobs at the ranch had been divided into *his* and *hers*. Cherry made everything *ours*.

"Where did you learn all these communal work ethics?" Billy asked as they each toweled off one of the twins after their bath.

"When there are eight kids in a household, everyone has to chip in and do their part," Cherry said. "And knowing there was at least one extra pair of hands to help made every job easier."

"And more fun," Billy said, as he picked up the twins, one in each arm, and headed toward their bedroom.

"And more fun," Cherry agreed as she turned down the twins' beds.

Billy set each twin on her bed and then sat down cross-legged on the floor between them. Cherry stood against the wall, her arms crossed around herself, watching them.

"Tell us a story," Raejean begged.

"Please, Daddy," Annie wheedled.

When the twins were younger and having children was still a novelty, Billy had often told them bedtime stories. As they had gotten older and his responsibilities on the ranch had become more pressing, Laura had been the one to put the girls to bed at night. He'd had to be satisfied with looking in on them after they were already asleep. Over the past year he had allowed a series of housekeepers to enjoy this precious time with his daughters.

Billy realized that he would probably be working on the bookkeeping right now if Cherry hadn't made everything so much fun that he had wanted to stay with them rather than retire to his office to work. He was grateful to her, but he couldn't tell her why without admitting he had been lax as a parent.

It shocked him to realize that maybe Penelope was right about him. Maybe he hadn't been a very good parent for his daughters over the past year. Maybe it was time to acknowledge that being a father meant more than planting the seeds in a woman that grew into children and earning the money that put food in their mouths, a roof over their heads, and clothes on their backs.

When he finished the story and his giggling girls were tucked in and kissed on their noses, he turned at last to find Cherry and realized that sometime during the reading of the bedtime story she had left the room.

"Good night, girls," he said as he turned out the light. "Sleep tight."

"Don't let the bedbugs bite!" they recited in chorus.

Billy headed downstairs in search of Cherry, anxious to thank her for making him aware of the priceless moments he had been missing with his daughters.

He knocked on the door to her room, but she wasn't there. He searched the house and finally found her sitting in one of the two rockers on the front porch. It was dark outside, and when he turned on the front porch light she said, "Please leave it off."

"All right," he said as he settled in the second rocker. "What are you doing sitting out here in the dark?"

"Thinking."

"About what?"

"About us. About why we got married." She pulled her feet up onto the rocker seat, circled her legs with her arms, and set her chin on her knees as she stared into the darkness. "We shouldn't have done it, Billy," she said softly.

"I disagree, Cherry. Especially after today."

She lifted her head and turned to stare at him. "I would think, if anything, today proved what a rotten mother I am. I wasn't going to tell you, but Annie and Raejean missed the bus this morning, so I had to take them there and I didn't know how to drive a stick shift and I forgot to make them lunches and then I let Annie eat too many marshmallows and then Mrs. Trask showed up at school because I wasn't here to get the call from the principal, and then Raejean ran off and the kitchen was a mess and supper wasn't ready and—''

Billy stood abruptly and lifted her out of the rocker and settled her in his lap as he sat back down. He felt the tension in her body and wanted desperately to ease the misery he had heard in her voice.

''So maybe you don't have the mechanics down. But you know everything about being a mother that really counts.''

''Like what?'' she said, her voice muffled because she had her mouth pressed against his throat.

''Like wanting them to be happy. Like caring what happens to them. Teaching them to do their share. Showing them the pleasure of doing something nice for somebody else. And showing me how much I've been missing by letting someone else try to be both parents, instead of doing my part.''

He felt her relax against him, felt her hand curl up behind his neck and thread into his hair. He liked the feel of her in his arms, liked the way she leaned on him.

''Thanks, Billy,'' she murmured. ''I want to be a helpmate for you.''

She sounded tired, half asleep. After the day she had described to him, it was no wonder. ''You are, Cherry,'' he said, pulling her close. ''You are.''

He only meant to give her a kiss of comfort. His intent wasn't the least bit amorous. He tipped her chin up with his forefinger and pressed soothing kisses on her closed eyelids, her freckled cheeks, and her nose. And one last kiss on her mouth.

Only he let himself linger a bit too long.

And Cherry returned the kiss. Her tongue made a long, lazy foray into his mouth.

His body reacted instantly, turning rock-hard. He groaned, almost in pain. He wanted her. Desperately. But he had agreed to wait.

"Cherry, please," he begged.

She didn't answer him one way or the other. He had to touch her, needed to touch her. He slid his hand up under her T-shirt and let his fingertips roam the silky flesh across her belly. His thumb caught under her breast.

He reached for the center clasp of her bra, holding his breath, hoping she wouldn't ask him to stop. He felt the clasp come free and huffed out a breath all at the same time.

She made a carnal sound as his hand closed over the warmth of her breast and gasped as his thumb flicked across the rigid nipple.

His mouth covered hers, and his tongue mimicked the sexual act as his hand palmed her flesh and then slid down between her legs. He cupped her and felt the heat and heard her moan.

His mouth slid down to her throat, sucking hard at the flesh as his thumb caressed her through a thin layer of denim, making her writhe in his arms.

"Billy, no!"

He froze, his breath rasping out through his open mouth, his body aching. He didn't try to stop her when she stumbled from his lap and grabbed at one of the porch pillars to hold herself upright. Her whole body was trembling with desire—or fear, he wasn't sure which.

"I'm sorry," she said. "I can't. I'm sorry."

Then she was gone.

Eight

Cherry spent the first month of her marriage trying desperately to win Raejean's and Annie's trust. And trying desperately not to think about how close she had come those first few days to making love with Billy.

She had felt warm and safe and secure in his arms. She had felt desired and cherished. She had felt the beginnings of passion—and torn herself from his embrace.

It was fear that had kept her from surrendering. Fear that she would begin to care too much. Fear that what she felt for him was illusion. Fear that what he felt for her was too ephemeral to last. If she gave herself to him body and soul, she would be lost. And when the marriage was over, she would die inside.

It was safer to keep her distance. That was the hard lesson she had learned as a child. She knew better than to trust anyone with her heart. If she gave it up to Billy, he would only break it.

But she wasn't strong enough to deny herself his touch entirely. She liked his kisses. She liked his caresses. And they were a necessary part of the charade she and Billy were playing out for the benefit of Mrs. Trask.

Of course, Mrs. Trask wasn't there each morning when Billy slipped up behind her while she was making coffee and nuzzled her neck and said in a husky voice, "Good morning, Cherry."

Mrs. Trask wasn't there when she turned and pressed herself against him, sieved her fingers into his thick, silky hair, and waited for his morning kiss.

Mrs. Trask wasn't there when Billy lowered his head and took her lips in a kiss as tender as anything Cherry had ever experienced, or when that same kiss grew into something so terrifyingly overwhelming that it left her breathless.

If Billy had asked her to yield entirely, she would likely have stopped allowing the kisses. But he seemed to be satisfied with what she was willing to give him. It wasn't until a month had passed that it dawned on Cherry that each morning Billy asked for a little more. And each morning she gave it to him.

A hand cupping her breast. The feel of his arousal against her belly. Drugging kisses that left her knees ready to buckle. Her hand pressed to the front of his fly to feel the length and the hardness of him. His mouth on her throat. Her robe eased aside, and his mouth on her naked breast.

The feelings were exquisite. Irresistible. Like Billy himself.

If physical seduction had been his only allure, she might have resisted him more successfully. But not only was she attracted to Billy physically, she liked and admired him, as well. He was a good father, a hard worker, a considerate helpmate. Cherry knew she was sliding down a slippery slope. She was in serious danger of complete surrender.

She tried not to think about Billy during the day. It was easy for great stretches of time to involve herself with Raejean and Annie and housekeeping and the chores in the barn she had taken over for Billy. And she had started night school to earn her high school diploma, and there was always homework to be finished. Her life was full and busy, and she felt useful and satisfied.

Most of the time.

But she could feel Billy's eyes on her in the evening after supper when they spent time with the children and gave them their baths. Watching her. Waiting for her to want him the way he wanted her.

The sexual tension between them had grown palpable. Her skin tingled at the mere thought of him touching her. Her breasts ached for the feel of his callused hands. Her blood raced when she saw him come through the door each evening, his washboard belly visible through his open shirt, his sinewy arms bared by rolled-up shirtsleeves, his muscular body fatigued from a day of hard labor.

And her heart went out to him when she saw his face, his dark eyes haunted by the stress of an imminent showdown in court with Mrs. Trask. Was it any wonder she wanted to hold out her arms to him and offer comfort?

As he shoved open the kitchen screen door, her thoughts became reality. Their eyes met and held for an instant, and Cherry knew that tonight she would give herself to him. Tonight she would offer him solace, even if it meant giving up her own peace of mind.

"Hi, Daddy," Raejean said as Billy settled his Stetson on a hat rack by the kitchen door.

"Hi, Daddy," Annie echoed.

Cherry felt a tightness in her chest as she saw the smile form on his face when he lifted the girls up into his arms and gave each of them a kiss on the nose. He loved them so very much. And there was a very real danger that he would lose them.

"How are my girls?" he asked. "What are you doing to keep busy now that school's over?"

"Cherry made us work!" Raejean said.

Billy raised his eyebrows. "Oh?"

"We had to help dig a garden behind the house."

"A garden?"

Cherry met Billy's surprised look and explained, "I thought it would be nice to have some fresh vegetables." Then she realized how presumptuous it was to assume she would still be around in the fall to harvest them.

"We had to plant flowers around the edge of the garden when we were done digging," Annie said.

"What kind of flowers?" Billy asked.

"Marigolds," Annie chirped. "It was fun, Daddy."

"Did you have fun, too, Raejean?" Billy asked.

"Maybe," Raejean conceded. "A little."

Cherry knew it had been an adjustment for Raejean and Annie to find themselves suddenly responsible for chores appropriate to their ages. Before Laura's death they had been too young, and the series of housekeepers had found it easier to do the work themselves than to involve the children. Cherry had explained to Billy that she wasn't there as a housekeeper, she was there as a surrogate mother. And she could best teach the girls the things they would need to know to manage a ranching household by involving them in every aspect of what she did.

It wasn't until she had come to live with Rebecca and Zach that Cherry had been included in precisely that way in the running of a household. In previous foster homes she had been more like a maid-of-all-work. In the Whitelaw home she had been part of a family in which each member did his or her part. She had learned the satisfaction to be had from contributing her fair share.

The more she put to good use the lessons Rebecca had taught her, the more she realized how much she had learned from her, the more grateful she felt for having been adopted into the Whitelaw family, and the more guilty she felt for having run away and married Billy instead of coming home and facing Zach and Rebecca the night she had been expelled.

There was no doubt she had been a difficult child to parent. The longer she was a stepparent, the more understanding she had of the other side of the fence. And the more appreciation she had for Zach and Rebecca's endless patience and love.

She knew she ought to tell them so.

But she couldn't face them and say on the one hand how much she appreciated all the things they had taught her, while on the other she was perpetrating the deceit involved in her temporary marriage to Billy Stonecreek.

So she had found excuses to avoid visiting them and reasons to keep her family from visiting her. Except for Jewel, who knew everything, and was quick to point out that Cherry was acting like an idiot and should simply call Zach and Rebecca and confess everything.

"They'll understand," Jewel had said. "And they'll forgive. And they'll still love you as much as ever. That's what parents do."

Cherry was finding that out for herself. Raejean still resented her and complained about nearly everything Cherry asked her to do, although she would eventually do it. Annie hadn't surrendered her trust to Cherry in loyalty to Raejean.

If her marriage to Billy had been a permanent thing, Cherry would have said time was on her side. It had taken more than a year for her barriers to come down with Zach and Rebecca, but in the face of all that love, they *had* come down. She needed to win Raejean's and Annie's trust before the court hearing—a matter of weeks. A great deal depended on her finding a way to break through the little girls' stubborn resistance.

They had long since broken through hers. She loved them both dearly, enough to know it was going to hurt a great deal when she was no longer a part of their lives.

"You got a letter today," she told Billy as he set the girls back on their feet. "It looks official."

Billy's face was grim as he went to the kitchen counter where she always left the mail and sorted through it. He picked up the envelope, looked at it, and set it back down again. "It can wait until after the kids are in bed."

Cherry understood why he was postponing the inevitable. But she knew he was as aware of it sitting there all evening as she was.

He hugged the girls so hard at bedtime that Annie protested, "I can't breathe, Daddy."

She knew he was afraid of losing them. So was she.

She walked ahead of him down the stairs and instead of heading for the porch rockers to relax for a few minutes before going back to work, she headed for the kitchen. Billy followed her.

She went directly to the stack of mail, found the letter she wanted, and handed it to him. "Read it."

He tore it open viciously, his teeth clenched tight enough to make a muscle in his jaw jerk. He read silently. Without a word, he handed the official-looking letter to her. "Read it."

She read quickly. The court date had been set for July 15. Billy was asked to appear and explain certain accusations that had been made against him that he was not a fit custodian for his children.

"Three weeks," he said bitterly. "Three lousy weeks before I have to appear in court and prove I'm a fit father. How the hell am I going to do that, Cherry? Tell me that? I can't make those nights in jail go away. And you can bet Penelope will make sure the judge knows that the mother I've provided for my children is an eighteen-year-old girl who used to be a juvenile delinquent.''

Cherry went white around the mouth. She hadn't expected his attack. It was useless to point out that he was the one who had suggested marriage. It didn't change the facts. ''What do you want to do, Billy? Do you want to annul the marriage? Would that help, do you think?''

''Oh, God, no!'' His arms closed tight around her. ''I'm sorry, Cherry. I didn't mean to suggest that any of this is your fault, or that you aren't a wonderful mother. You are. Raejean and Annie are lucky to have you. Only...''

''Only I have been a juvenile delinquent.''

''And I've spent a few nights in jail,'' Billy said. ''Nobody's perfect, Cherry. We simply have to convince the judge that all that behavior is in the past. That right now we're the best possible parents for two little girls who've lost their mother, and whose grandmother is a bit misguided.''

''Is that what she is?'' Cherry asked, her lips twisting wryly.

''She misses her daughter, Cherry. She's still grieving. But that doesn't mean I'm going to give her my children to replace the one she lost,'' Billy said, his voice hard, his eyes flinty.

''Raejean still doesn't like me,'' Cherry pointed out. ''What is the judge going to make of that?''

Billy's brow furrowed between his eyes. "I don't know, Cherry. He'll have to understand that we're all still making adjustments. He'll have to see that you're doing the best you can."

She took a deep breath and said, "I couldn't bear to see you lose them, Billy."

"I won't. I can't." He paused at the realization that the court had the power to take his children away from him before repeating, "I won't."

His arms tightened painfully around her, and she knew he was holding on to her because he was afraid of losing them. When his mouth came seeking hers—seeking solace, as she had known he would—she gave it to him.

"I need you," he said in a guttural voice. "I need you, Cherry."

"I'm yours, Billy," she answered him. "I'm all yours."

He picked her up and carried her to her room, shoving open the bedroom door with his hip and laying her on the bed. He turned on the bedside lamp and sat down beside her.

"I want to see you. I want to feel your flesh against mine," he said as he tore off her T-shirt and threw it across the room. He had her bra unclasped a second later and it was gone, leaving her bared to him from the waist up.

He stopped to look at what he had. "No freckles here," he mused as a callused finger circled her breast. "Just this rosy crest," he finished as his mouth closed on her.

Her hands tangled in his hair and held him as he suckled her. Her body arched with pleasure as his hand slipped down between her legs to hold the heat and the heart of her.

Cherry had endured weeks of teasing foreplay. Now she wanted what had been denied her. "Please, Billy. Please." She shoved at his shirt, wanting to feel his flesh against her fingertips. She reached for his belt buckle and undid it with trembling fingers and then undid the button and slid down the zipper on his jeans. Billy copied everything she did.

When her hand slid beneath his briefs to reach for him, his did the same beneath her panties.

They stopped and looked at each other and grinned.

"Gotcha," Billy said as he slid a finger deep inside her. She was wet and slick, and he added another finger to the first.

Cherry groaned.

Her gaze trailed down to where her hand disappeared inside Billy's briefs. She tightened her grasp and slid her hand up and down the hard length of him.

Billy groaned.

Their mouths merged, their tongues mimicking the sexual act as their hands kept up their teasing titillation.

Suddenly it wasn't enough. Cherry wasn't sure which of them shoved at the other's jeans first, but it wasn't long before both of them were naked. A moment after that, Billy was inside her.

They both went still.

It felt like she had found her other half. Now she was whole.

Cherry looked up into Billy's dark eyes and saw a wealth of emotion. Too many feelings. More than were safe. She closed her eyes against them.

"Look at me, Cherry," Billy said.

She slowly raised her lids and gazed at him with wonder.

He loves me, she thought. *I never dreamed...I never imagined...*

She waited for the words, but he never said them.

And she knew why. She didn't love him back. She wouldn't allow herself to love him. He knew the rules. It was to be a safe, temporary marriage.

Her eyes slid closed again as his mouth covered hers, hungry, needy. For the first time in her life she was grateful for her height, which made them fit together so perfectly that they could be joined at the hip and their mouths still meet for a soul-searching kiss. She felt the passion rise, felt her body shiver and shudder under the onslaught of his desire.

His body moved slowly at first, the tension building equally slowly, until it was unbearable, until she writhed beneath him, desperate for release.

"Please, Billy," she cried. "Please!"

She heard a savage sound deep in his throat as his body surged against hers, as he fought the inevitable climax, wanting to prolong the pleasure.

She felt her body tensing, thrusting against his, seeking the heaven he promised, until they found it, his seed spilling into her at last.

His weight was welcome, comforting, as he lowered his exhausted, sweat-slick body onto hers, their chests still heaving to gather breath to support their labored bodies, their heartbeats still pounding to carry blood to straining vessels.

Eventually, as their breathing slowed and their hearts returned to normal, Billy slid to her side and spooned her bottom against his groin. His hand curled around her breast as though it were the most natural place in the world for it to be. "Thanks, Cherry. I needed that. You," he amended.

It was more than she was willing to admit, so she remained mute. She was content to lie in his arms, saying nothing, enjoying the closeness.

It was during this quiet aftermath that she realized they had used no protection. They both knew better. Under the circumstances, a pregnancy could be disastrous. "Billy," she murmured.

"Hmm."

"We didn't use anything."

"Hmm?"

"To keep me from getting pregnant."

His stiffening body revealed his distress. "I should have asked. I should have—"

She turned in his arms and put her fingertips against his lips. "It's the wrong time of the month, I think."

"You think?"

"If there is a safe time," she amended, "this is probably it."

"Thank God," he said.

Even though she knew rationally that it was in both of their interests for her not to get pregnant, it was still irksome to see the amount of relief on Billy's face. "I guess you don't want any more children," she said.

"It isn't that," he said. "I always wanted more kids. But Laura . . ."

She remembered that Laura couldn't have any more. Only, that wasn't what Billy said next.

"Laura wasn't supposed to get pregnant because it was dangerous."

She felt him shudder and a thought occurred to her. "Are you saying she got pregnant anyway?"

He paused so long she didn't think he was going to answer her. At last he said, "Yes."

"What happened? To the baby, I mean?"

"She miscarried. Twice."

He pulled her close so his chin rested on her head, and she couldn't see his eyes. But she could feel him trembling and hear his convulsive swallow.

"The second time it happened I told her that if she didn't stop trying to get pregnant, I'd refuse to sleep with her anymore. I didn't want to take the chance of losing her. She meant too much to me, more than any baby ever could."

Another swallow.

"She was furious with me. She said she had promised me a houseful of kids, and she knew I couldn't be happy with just the twins. I told her the twins were enough. But she didn't believe me.

"The truth was, she had this insane idea that a woman who couldn't have kids wasn't a real woman. She refused to stop trying to get pregnant, despite the risk to her health. So I told her I was through arguing. I wasn't going to sleep with her again until she changed her mind and agreed to be sensible."

He shuddered.

"She went stomping out of the house, furiously angry, and got into the car. And...and she was killed."

"Oh, my God," Cherry breathed. "And you're not really sure whether it was an accident, or whether she killed herself on purpose, is that it?"

"She wouldn't kill herself. Not because of something like that. She wouldn't. It was an accident."

Cherry wasn't sure who he was trying to convince, himself or her.

"All Penelope saw the year before she died was Laura's despondency over the first miscarriage," Billy continued. "Penelope knew we'd been arguing a lot around the time of Laura's death, although she didn't know what we'd been arguing about. Laura didn't tell her about the miscarriage—probably because she knew her mother would be on my side."

"Why didn't you tell Mrs. Trask what had happened?" Cherry asked.

"It was none of her business!" Billy retorted. "It was between me and my wife."

"Maybe if she understood why—"

"It's over and done with now."

"Perhaps if you explained—"

"Laura's dead. There's no bringing her back."

And he wasn't sure he wasn't to blame, Cherry realized. No wonder he had gotten into so many fights in the year since Laura's death. He had been in pain, with no way of easing it. Because he would never know for sure what had happened.

"It wasn't your fault she died," Cherry said quietly.

"How do you know that?" he snarled.

"You were right. It wasn't safe for her to continue getting pregnant. You had to take a stand."

"I should have found some other way to say no."

"Hindsight is always better. You did the best you could at the time."

"That's supposed to make me feel better?"

She leaned back to look into his troubled eyes and saw the need in him to strike out against the pain.

There were other ways of easing it. She laid her hand against his cheek and said, "You're a good man, Billy. You never meant for her to be hurt. Whether it was an accident ... or not ... Laura was responsible for what happened."

"I want to believe that," he said. "I try to believe that. But..."

"Believe it," she whispered as her lips sought his.

His arms surrounded her like iron bands, and his mouth sought hers like a thirsting man who finds an oasis in the desert. He was inside her moments later, needing the closeness, needing the comfort she offered, the surcease from endless pain.

She held him in her arms as he loved her and crooned to him that everything would be all right. That he was a good man and a good father and he shouldn't blame himself anymore for what wasn't his fault.

He spilled himself inside her with a cry that was almost anguish. He slipped to the side and pulled her to him, holding her close with strong arms that promised always to keep her safe.

She knew it was wrong to trust in him. He would betray her in the end. Unfortunately, the heart doesn't always obey the dictates of the more reasonable head.

I love him, she thought. And then, *I can't love him. I shouldn't love him. I'd be a fool to love him.*

They fell asleep, their bodies entangled, their souls enmeshed, their hearts confused.

Nine

Over the next three weeks the twins sensed the growing tension in Billy, and their behavior grew worse instead of better. Cherry tried to be understanding, but she was under a great deal of pressure, as well, since she had to study for night school finals, which she couldn't afford to fail.

Things came to a head the day before the court hearing, when Cherry asked Raejean for the third time to take her cookie and juice snack back to the kitchen to eat it.

"I don't have to do what you say," Raejean said. "You're not my mother!"

"I'm the one in charge," Cherry replied, using her last ounce of patience to keep her voice level. "And I say you have to get that juice out of the living room. If it spills in here, it'll ruin the furniture."

Cherry couldn't imagine what had possessed Laura to put silk and satin fabrics in a ranch living room. It wasn't a place to look at; they actually lived in it. If it had been up to her, she would have put protective covers on the furniture long ago to save the delicate fabrics from everyday wear and tear. When she had broached the subject to Billy, he had said, "We live here. If the furniture gets dirty, it gets dirty."

Cherry didn't figure that included spilling grape juice on white satin. So she insisted, "Take that juice into the kitchen, Raejean. Now!"

"Oh, all right!" Raejean huffed. "Come on, Annie. Let's go."

"I'm watching Sesame Street," Annie protested from her seat beside Raejean on the couch.

Raejean pinched her. "Come on. If I have to go, you have to go."

"Raejean," Cherry warned. "Leave Annie be. Take your glass and go."

Raejean shot Cherry a mutinous look as she snatched at the glass on the end table, accidentally knocking it over—right onto the arm of the couch.

The two of them stared, horrified, as the grape juice soaked into the white satin, leaving a huge purple blotch.

"Oh, no!" Cherry cried. She looked for something to sop up the mess, but there was nothing handy. And by then the couch had soaked up the juice like a sponge.

"It's all your fault," Raejean cried, tears welling in her eyes. "If you hadn't been yelling at me, I wouldn't have spilled it."

"Daddy's going to be *really* mad," Annie whispered as she abandoned Sesame Street to ogle the growing stain.

"Go to your room," Cherry said. "Both of you!"

"I didn't do anything," Annie protested.

"We don't have to do what you say!" Raejean said. "Do we, Annie?"

Annie looked uncertain, and Raejean pinched her again.

"Ow!" she said. "Stop it, Raejean."

"Stop it, both of you!" Cherry cried. She knew she had lost control, but she wasn't sure how to get it back. "Apologize to your sister, Raejean."

"I don't have to. Tell her, Annie. Tell her Nana's going to be taking care of us from now on, so we don't have to do what Cherry says anymore."

Cherry couldn't believe what she was hearing. "Who said your grandmother's going to be taking care of you from now on?"

"Nana did."

"When?" Cherry said.

"When she called on the phone."

"When was that?" Cherry demanded.

"This morning, when you were in the shower. She said that after tomorrow she's going to be taking care of us, and we'll get to play in her pool and Grampa's buying us a new dollhouse and we won't have to do chores anymore, either," she announced.

Cherry stared at Raejean, aghast. She didn't know what to say. The little girl had no idea what Mrs. Trask really intended. She didn't seem to realize that going to live with her grandmother meant leaving her father for good. And Cherry had no intention of frightening her by explaining it.

She was furious with Mrs. Trask but resisted the urge to criticize her in front of her granddaughters. She was way out of her depth and drowning fast. She needed help.

To Cherry's surprise, the name and face that came to mind wasn't Billy's. Or even Jewel's. It was Rebecca's.

She wanted her mother.

"Let's go," she said suddenly.

"Go where?" Raejean asked suspiciously.

"To see your other grandmother."

Both girls stared at her with wide eyes.

"We have another grandmother?" Annie said.

"Uh-huh. You sure do."

"Who is she?" Raejean asked. "Where does she live?"

"Her name is Rebecca Whitelaw, and she lives on a ranch called Hawk's Pride. It isn't far from here. Shall we go? It's either that, or go to your room. You choose."

There was no contest, and Cherry wasted no time getting the girls into the pickup and driving to the adobe ranch house at Hawk's Pride that she had called home for the previous four years. Since Camp Littlehawk was under way, she knew where to look for Rebecca. Sure enough, she found her working with the novice riders at the corral. Raejean and Annie raced ahead of her to stand gaping at the lucky horseback riders.

"That's good, Jamie," Rebecca encouraged, one foot perched on the lowest rung of the wooden corral. "Let the pony know who's boss."

"I suppose that's good advice for parents dealing with children, too," Cherry said as she joined Rebecca.

"Cherry! What a wonderful surprise! Ted, would you watch the children for a few minutes while I speak with my daughter?"

Cherry noticed that Ted was on crutches. That didn't surprise her. Rebecca often found people in need and offered them a helping hand. Cherry was sure Ted was great with kids or horses or both. It always worked out that way. Rebecca's faith in people had never been proven wrong. It was that same goodheartedness that had led Rebecca to rescue a rebellious fourteen-year-old juvenile delinquent and adopt her as her own.

"I'd like you to meet your new granddaughters," Cherry said as Rebecca took the few steps to reach the twins. They were standing on the bottom rail of the corral with their arms hanging over the top.

"Raejean, Annie, I'd like you to meet your Grandma 'Becca." 'Becca was what Jewel had called Rebecca when Jewel was a child. It was also a fond nickname Zach used when he was teasing her. And it was the first thing that came to mind when Cherry searched for a name the little girls could use to address their new grandmother.

Raejean and Annie turned lively black eyes on Rebecca.

"Are you really our grandmother?" Raejean asked.

"Yes," Rebecca said with a smile.

"Are you going to give us cookies and milk, like Nana?" Annie asked.

"I'll even help you bake the cookies, if you like," Rebecca said. "If you'll tell me which one of you is which."

"I'm Annie," Raejean said. "And this is Raejean," she said, pointing to her shyer twin.

"Raejean," Cherry warned.

"Aw, Cherry." She hesitated before admitting, "I'm really Raejean, and this is really Annie."

"Pleased to meet you both," Rebecca said. "It's going to be fun having grandchildren come to visit."

"Will you let us ride horses, too?" Raejean asked, eyeing the children on horseback enviously.

"Would you like to ride one now?"

Raejean's and Annie's faces lit up as though they had been given the key to heaven. "Oh, yes!" they said in unison.

It didn't take long to get ponies saddled and send the girls into the ring with the other children to be supervised by Ted.

As soon as the twins were settled, Rebecca said, "All right, Cherry. Spit it out. What's wrong?"

"Everything," Cherry admitted. She felt like crying suddenly. The whole weight of the world had been on her shoulders for the past seven weeks, and it was as though with that one admission she had shifted the burden to her mother.

"Tell me about it," Rebecca said.

And Cherry did. About why she and Billy had married and the awful wedding and the twins' resentment, how Mrs. Trask was manipulating the children's feelings, and how scared she was that Billy would lose his children.

"What about you? Would it hurt you to lose them?"

Cherry hadn't even let herself think about the possibility. When she did, she felt a terrible ache in her chest. "Yes. Oh, yes. I'd miss them terribly. As much trouble as they are, I love them dearly."

Rebecca smiled. "So what can I do to help?"

Cherry shoved a hand through her tumble of red curls and let out a gusty sigh. "I'm not sure. Could you and Zach just be there in court tomorrow? Would that be possible?"

"Oh, darling, of course we'll be there. Is that all? Are you sure there isn't something else I could do to help?"

"I think you've already done it," Cherry said.

"Done what?"

"Taught me to believe in love again."

"Oh, darling..."

Cherry saw the tears in her mother's eyes and felt her throat tighten until it hurt. "I owe you so much... Mother." She gave a sobbing laugh and said, "There, I said it. Mother. Oh, God, why did I wait so long?"

It had taken being a mother herself to understand the tremendous gift Zach and Rebecca had given her. She could hardly see Rebecca through the blur of tears, and when she blinked, she realized Rebecca had her arms open wide. She grasped her around the waist and held on tight.

Cherry refused her mother's invitation to stay for dinner. "Billy and Zach—Daddy—aren't comfortable enough around each other yet. I'd rather give them time to get to know each other better before we show up for supper."

"All right. Whatever you think best. You can count on us to be in court tomorrow to support you both."

"Thanks, Mother. That means a lot."

"I wasn't sure before that you were ready for marriage and all its responsibilities," Rebecca said. "This visit has reassured me."

"That I'm ready for marriage?"

"That you're ready for whatever life offers. Be happy, Cherry. That's all I can ask."

Cherry smiled. "I'll try, Mom."

"Mom. I like that," Rebecca said. "Mom feels even better than Mother."

"Yeah, Mom," Cherry agreed with a cheeky grin. "It does."

Cherry spent the rest of the afternoon floating on air. She had never felt so confident. She had never been so certain that everything would turn out all right. Her youthful optimism remained firmly in place until Billy was late arriving home for supper. She waited an hour for him before she finally fed the girls and sent them upstairs to play.

She put a plate of food in the oven to stay warm while she cleaned up the kitchen. She still wasn't worried. Billy had been late once or twice before when some work had needed to be finished before dark.

But sundown came and went without any sign of Billy.

Cherry told herself, as she bathed the twins, that there was probably some good reason for the delay. Maybe he was working hard to make up for the fact he would be in court all day tomorrow. Maybe the truck had broken down and he had needed to walk home.

Maybe he had an accident. Maybe he's lying hurt or dying somewhere while you've been blithely assuming everything is fine.

Cherry silenced the voice that told her disaster had struck. Nothing could have happened to Billy. He was strong and had quick reflexes, and he knew the dangers of the kind of work he did. He was fine.

But he was very late.

Cherry read the girls two bedtime stories, thinking he would show up at any minute to tease and tickle them and kiss them good-night.

"Where's Daddy?" Raejean asked when Cherry said it was time to turn out the light.

"Isn't he coming home?" Annie asked.

"Of course he's coming home. He just had some errands to run. As soon as he arrives, he'll come and kiss you good-night. Go to sleep now."

She turned out the light and was almost out of the room when Raejean whispered, "Is Daddy going away?"

Cherry turned the light back on. Both Raejean and Annie stared back at her with frightened eyes. *Damn Mrs. Trask and her phone calls,* Cherry thought. She crossed and sat beside Raejean and brushed the bangs away and kissed her forehead reassuringly.

"Your daddy isn't going anywhere. He'll be right here when you wake up in the morning."

"Nana said Daddy might be going away," Raejean confessed." I don't want him to leave."

"Neither do I," Annie whimpered.

"Oh, my dear ones," Cherry said. She lifted a sobbing Raejean into her arms and carried her over to Annie's bed, then slid an arm around each girl and rocked them against her. "Don't worry. Everything's going to be fine. Your Daddy's not going anywhere. And neither am I."

"Are you going to be our mother forever?" Annie asked.

Cherry was struck dumb by the question. She realized the folly of her promise that she wasn't going anywhere. She and Billy had a temporary marriage. She had no right to presume he would want it to continue any longer than necessary to convince the court to let him keep his children.

She was forced to admit the truth to herself.

She didn't want the marriage to end. She wanted to stay married to Billy. She wanted to be the twins' mother forever. All she had to do was convince Billy to let her stay.

When he showed up. If he ever did.

"Why don't we ask your daddy when he comes home if it's all right with him for me to be your mother forever," she answered Annie at last. "Would that be all right?"

"I guess," Annie said. "If you're sure he's coming home."

"I'm sure," Cherry said.

That seemed to assuage the worst of their fear, and she managed to get them tucked in again. As she was turning out the light, Raejean said, "Cherry?"

"What is it, Raejean?"

"I don't want you to leave, either."

Cherry smiled. "Thanks, Raejean. That means a lot to me."

She rose up on one elbow and said, "I'm sorry about spilling grape juice on the couch. You don't think Daddy came home and saw it while we were gone and got *really* mad, do you?"

Her heart went out to the child. "No, Raejean, I don't think it's anything you did that's making your father late getting home. I'm sure he's been delayed by business. Go to sleep now. Before you know it, he'll be waking you up to kiss you good-night."

As she was closing the door, Cherry heard Annie whisper, "That's silly. Why is Daddy going to wake us up to kiss us good-night?"

"So we'll know he's home, dummy," Raejean explained scornfully.

"Oh," Annie whispered back. "All right."

Cherry headed downstairs hoping that Billy would arrive to fulfill her promise and waken the twins with a kiss.

As the night passed and he didn't return, she began to worry in earnest. The worst thing was, she had no idea where he might have gone. She made up her mind to wait until midnight before she called the police to report him missing. That's when the bars in town closed.

Not that she believed for one second that he had gone to a bar. Not with everything on the line the way it was. Not with everything he did subject to intense scrutiny in the courtroom. Not as determined as he was to keep custody of his children in the face of his mother-in-law's clutching grasp for them.

She sat in the dark on the front porch step, waiting for him to come home. At five minutes before midnight she saw a pair of headlights coming down the dirt road that led to the house. Her heart began to pound.

Surely it was Billy. Surely it was him and not someone coming to tell her he had been hurt.

The vehicle was headed for the back of the house, moving too fast for safety. She ran through the house, turned on the back porch light and slammed her way out the back door. She was there when the pickup skidded to a stop.

When she saw it was Billy's truck, she released a breath of air she hadn't realized she had been holding. The relief turned quickly to anger when Billy stepped out of the truck and she saw his face. One eye was swollen almost closed and his lip had a cut on one side.

"You've been fighting!" She gasped as he began to weave his way unsteadily toward her. "You're drunk!" she accused. "How could you, Billy? How could you?"

"I'm not drunk!" he said. "I've just got a couple of cracked ribs that are giving me hell."

She quickly moved to support him. "What happened? Where have you been? Who did this to you?"

She felt him slump against her. "Aw, Cherry, I don't believe I let this happen. Not the day before I have to go to court. The judge'll never understand."

"Forget the judge. Explain this to me."

"I went to town to get some supplies at the hardware store and ran into that Ray character, the one who took you to the prom."

"Ray did this to you?" she asked incredulously.

"Him and three of his friends."

"But why?"

"It doesn't matter why. Or it won't to the judge. All he'll see is that I've been fighting again. Lord, Cherry, I hurt. Inside and out."

"Come on in to the kitchen and let me bind your ribs," Cherry said. "Maybe I can get the swelling down in your eye, so it won't look so bad tomorrow."

"Maybe I can say I'm sick and get a postponement," Billy suggested.

"Is it possible the Trasks won't find out about the fight? Did the police come?" she asked.

"They were there," Billy said.

"But you weren't arrested?" Cherry said. "That must mean something. I mean, that you weren't at fault."

"I wanted to fight, all right," Billy said flatly. "And I'd do it again."

"Don't say things like that. You can't keep getting into fights, Billy. Not if you want to keep custody of your girls. What could be so important it was worth risking your girls to fight about?" she demanded.

He didn't answer her, but that could have been because he was too busy hissing in a breath as she administered antiseptic to the cuts on his face. She eased the torn shirt off his shoulders and saw the bruises on his ribs. They must have kicked him when he was down.

"Where have you been all night, if you weren't in a bar somewhere drinking?" Cherry asked.

"I went to the stock pond to sit and think," he said.

"While you were thinking, did it occur to you that I'd be worried," Cherry asked archly.

"I'm sorry, Cherry. I lost track of the time."

He sat stoically while she strapped his ribs. But the light had gone out of his eyes. He had already given up. He had already conceded the battle to Penelope.

"You aren't going to lose tomorrow," she said to him. "You can tell the judge a bull stomped you, or—"

Billy snorted. "Stomped on my eye? Forget it, Cherry. You know as well as I do that my fight with Penelope is over before it's begun."

"I refuse to accept that!" Cherry snapped back. "You're a good father. You love your children, and you provide a stable home for them."

"That isn't enough."

"What more can the judge ask?" Cherry demanded.

Billy reached up gingerly and brushed his hair out of his eyes. "I don't know. You can believe there'll be something Penelope can offer that I can't."

"There's *nothing* she can give them that you can't," Cherry said fiercely. "And there's something you can give them that no one else can."

"What?"

"Love. A parent's love. Don't discount it, Billy. It's a powerful thing."

She saw the doubt in his eyes. He wanted to believe her, but he was afraid to let his hopes get too high. She lowered her lips to his, tender, as gentle as she had ever been. She brushed at the hank of hair that had fallen once more on his forehead. "You're going to win, Billy. Believe it."

He took her hand and pressed her palm against his lips. "Thanks, Cherry. I needed to hear that."

But she saw he didn't completely believe it. He believed this was the beginning of the end. He believed he was going to lose his children. That he was going to lose her. She could feel it in the way he clung to her hand.

She pulled herself free, unwilling to indulge in his despair.

"The girls were worried about you," she said as she scurried around fixing an ice pack for his eye. "I promised them you would wake them up to kiss them good-night so they would know you got home all right."

"I'll go do that now," he said, groaning as he got to his feet, the ice pack pressed against his eye.

"Don't fall coming back downstairs," she said.

He turned and looked at her. He was in no condition to make love to her, and for a second she thought he was going to refuse to come back downstairs and join her in bed. But he nodded his head in acquiescence.

"I'll be down in a few minutes."

Cherry hurried to finish her ablutions and ready herself for bed before Billy came to her room. The sexiest nightgown she owned was a football jersey,

JOAN JOHNSTON 163

and she quickly slipped it over her head. She was naked underneath it.

She pulled the covers down and slipped under them to wait for him. She left the light burning, because she knew he liked to watch her as they made love.

It didn't take her long to realize, once Billy entered her room and began undressing himself, that he needed help. She got out of bed and came to him, sick at heart at this reminder of the fight that might cost him his children.

She took her time undressing him, kissing his flesh as she exposed it. Shoulders. Chest. Belly. She sat him down and pulled off his boots and socks and made him stand again so she could unbuckle his belt and unzip his jeans and pull them off. By the time he was naked, he was also obviously aroused.

"Lie down," she coaxed. "You're hurt. Let me do all the work."

She had never said she loved Billy in words. But she showed him with her mouth and hands and body. She eased herself down on his shaft, and when he arched his body into hers, said, "Lie still. I'll move for both of us."

She did, riding him like a stallion, never giving him a rest, until both of them were breathing hard and slick with sweat. She pushed him to the brink, brought him back, and took him there again. Until at last she rode him home.

He was already asleep, his breathing deep and even, by the time she slipped to his side, reached over to turn out the light, and snuggled against him.

"You'll win, Billy," she whispered into the darkness. "You have to win. Because I love you and Raejean and Annie. And I can't bear to give you up."

She felt his arm tighten around her.

At first she was terrified because she thought he must have heard her. Then she realized it was a reflexive move. He had reached for her in his sleep and pulled her close.

"You're not going to lose me, Billy," she murmured against his throat. "I'm not going anywhere."

His body relaxed, and she closed her eyes to sleep.

Ten

The day of the hearing dawned fly-buzzing hot, as though to deny the cloud of disaster that loomed over their heads. In the bright sunshine Billy's face looked even worse than it had the night before. His left eye was swollen nearly shut, and the myriad bruises had taken on a rainbow of colors—pink, yellow and purple. He walked stiffly up the courthouse steps, like an old man, an occasional wince revealing what even that effort cost him in pain.

Cherry had put on a simple, flowered cotton dress with a Peter Pan collar she often wore to church. It made her look every bit as young as she was. Billy was dressed in a dark suit that fit his broad shoulders like a glove and made him into a dangerous, imposing stranger.

The twins bounced along beside them in matching dresses and pigtails, chattering like magpies, excited by the prospect of going on a picnic after the court hearing was over. Cherry chattered back at them, putting on a cheery false front to prove she wasn't as frightened as she was.

She and Billy had exchanged very few words since waking that morning, but their eyes had met often, communicating a wealth of information.

I feel awful.

I can see that. You look like you got stomped by something mean.

What if I say something wrong? What if I can't convince the judge to let me keep my kids?

Everything will be all right.

What if it isn't? What will I do?

I'm here for you, Billy.

I'm scared, Cherry.

So am I.

I'm glad you're here with me.

He reached out to take her hand, clutching it so tightly it hurt, as they entered the courtroom. The instant the twins saw their grandparents sitting at a table at the front of the courtroom with two men dressed in expensive suits, they went racing down the aisle to greet them.

"Hi, Nana," Raejean said, giving her grandmother a hug. Mrs. Trask wore a sleek designer suit that shouted wealth, her short-cropped, silvery-white hair perfectly coiffed.

"Hi, Grandpa," Annie said, getting a sound hug from her grandfather. Mr. Trask sported a double-breasted wool blend suit, his pale blond hair cut short on top and trimmed high over his ears.

The adults exchanged not a word, but their eyes spoke volumes.

Animosity from Mrs. Trask.

Antagonism from Billy.

Anguish from Cherry.

"Raejean. Annie. Come sit over here," Billy ordered.

Reluctantly the girls left their grandparents and came to sit beside Billy and Cherry across the courtroom.

Billy's attorney had already suggested that Billy compromise with Mr. and Mrs. Trask and give them partial custody of the children. The lawyer had warned that with their duo of legal experts, the Trasks would very likely win full custody if Billy insisted on fighting them in court.

"Are you ready, Mr. Stonecreek?" Billy's lawyer asked as Billy and Cherry joined him.

"I'm ready." Billy knew his lawyer believed they were fighting a lost cause. But he wasn't willing to give up his children without clawing for them tooth and nail.

Billy turned to find the source of a small commotion at the back of the courtroom. "Cherry, look."

Cherry looked and felt tears prickle behind her eyes. Her whole family was trooping into the courtroom. Zach and Rebecca, Rolleen, Jewel, Avery, Jake, Frannie, Rabbit, and Colt. She knew what it meant at that moment to be part of a family. They were there for her.

"Thank you," she mouthed.

Her mother smiled encouragement. Zach nodded. Colt grinned and gave her a thumbs-up, while Jewel mouthed back, "We're with you, Cherry."

At that moment the judge entered the courtroom, and the bailiff called, "All rise."

Cherry stood and reached for Billy's hand as he reached for hers. They stood grim-lipped, stark-eyed, waiting for the worst, hoping for the best.

"In the interest of keeping this hearing as open and frank as we can get it," the judge began, "I think the minor children should wait outside. Is there someone who can take care of them?"

Jewel popped up in back. "I will, Your Honor."

"Very well. The children will leave the courtroom and remain outside until I call for them."

"Why do we have to leave, Daddy?" Raejean asked, her brow furrowed.

"Because the judge said so," Billy answered.

"I don't want to go," Annie said, clinging to Cherry's skirt.

"It's all right, Annie," Cherry said. "It's only for a little while. We'll all be together again soon."

She hoped.

Cherry prayed that the girls wouldn't make a scene in front of the judge, proving Cherry and Billy couldn't control their children. To her immense relief, they allowed Jewel to take their hands and lead them from the courtroom.

"This is a hearing to decide whether Mr. Stonecreek's two minor children should be taken away from him and given to their grandparents," the judge began solemnly. "I would like the petitioners to explain in their own words why they are seeking custody of their grandchildren."

"It's simple, Your Honor," Mrs. Trask said as she rose to her feet. "Billy Stonecreek is an inadequate and irresponsible parent who is doing irreparable harm to my grandchildren by neglecting them. He also happens to be a drunken brawler without an ounce of self-respect. It's a well-known fact that his kind can't hold their liquor."

"His kind?" the judge inquired.

"Billy Stonecreek's mother was an Indian, Your Honor," Mrs. Trask replied disdainfully.

The judge's brows arrowed down between his eyes, but all he said was, "Please continue."

"My former son-in-law has instigated several free-for-alls over the past year since my daughter's death, for which he has been repeatedly jailed. As you can plainly see from the condition of his face, he hasn't reformed his behavior over time.

"He has subjected my granddaughters to a series of housekeepers who come and go. His latest act of idiocy was to marry an eighteen-year-old high school dropout, who was a juvenile delinquent herself."

Billy had remained silent during Penelope's attack on him. When she started on Cherry, he couldn't sit still for it. "Wait one damn minute—"

"Sit down, Mr. Stonecreek," the judge admonished. "You'll have a chance to speak your piece."

Penelope shot Billy a smug smile and continued. "This pitiful excuse for a father doesn't have the time, money, or inclination to give his children the things they need. On the other hand, Mr. Trask and I are ready, willing, and able to provide a secure and stable home for our grandchildren."

"Is there anything else?" the judge asked.

Mrs. Trask hesitated before she said, "I believe Billy Stonecreek is responsible for my daughter, Laura's, death, Your Honor."

The judge raised a disbelieving brow.

"He didn't kill her with his bare hands," Mrs. Trask said. "But he made her so unhappy that...that she took her own life."

Cherry bounced up and said, "That's not true, Your Honor!"

The judge made a disgruntled sound. "Young lady—"

"Please, Your Honor. You have to let me speak," Cherry pleaded.

The judge turned to Mrs. Trask and said, "Are you finished, Mrs. Trask?"

"I am, Your Honor." She sat down as regally as a queen reclaiming her throne.

"Very well, then. Proceed, Mrs. Stonecreek."

"It simply isn't true that Billy is responsible for Laura's death."

"Cherry, don't," Billy muttered.

Cherry looked Billy in the eye and said, "I have to tell them, Billy. It's the only way."

· When he lowered his gaze, she turned to face the judge. "Laura Stonecreek didn't commit suicide, Your Honor. She was involved in a tragic automobile accident. She was unhappy, all right—because she wanted to have more children, but wasn't medically able to carry another child to term. On the day she had her fatal accident, Laura miscarried a child for the second time."

An audible gasp could be heard from the other table.

"Billy didn't want her to take the risk of getting pregnant anymore. When Laura left the house that day she was despondent, but not because Billy didn't love her enough. It was because he loved her too much to take the chance of losing her by getting her pregnant again.

"Billy Stonecreek is the most gentle, most kind, and considerate man I know. He's a wonderful father to his girls, and they love him dearly. If you could only see him with them, giving them a bath, reading a story to them, kissing them good-night. They trust him to take care of them always. It would be a travesty to separate them."

"What you say is all to the good, Mrs. Stonecreek," the judge said. "But I'm concerned about your husband's propensity to physical violence. I'm especially concerned to see his condition today. I would think he would have avoided this sort of behavior, when he knew he would be appearing before this court."

Cherry felt miserable. Billy had refused to tell her why he had gotten into another fight. And he had said he would do it again. She could understand the judge's point. There was nothing she could say to defend Billy, except, "He's a good man, Your Honor. He loves his children. Please don't take them away from him."

"Excuse me, Your Honor."

Cherry turned at the sound of her father's voice. Zach was standing, waiting to be recognized by the judge.

"What is it, Zach?"

Cherry was surprised to hear the judge call her father by his first name until she remembered what Billy had said when he married her. The Whitelaws were well known around this part of Texas. It appeared Zach had a personal acquaintance with the judge.

"I can explain the cause of Billy's most recent altercation, if the court will allow it."

The two lawyers conferred hastily at the Trasks' table before one rose to say, "I object, Your Honor. Mr. Whitelaw has no standing to get involved in this case."

"I'm the grandfather of those little girls, too, Your Honor," Zach said. "My daughter hasn't adopted them yet, but that's only a formality. I know she loves them as though they were already her own."

Cherry's throat thickened with emotion.

"I see no reason why I shouldn't allow Mr. Whitelaw to make his point, Counsel," the judge said. "Especially in light of the consequences if I rule against Mr. Stonecreek. I'd like to hear an explanation for this most recent fight—if there is one. Go ahead, Zach."

"First let me say that I did not initially approve of my daughter's marriage. I thought she was too young, and I knew Billy Stonecreek's reputation for getting into trouble. I thought he would be a bad influence on her."

Cherry felt her heart sinking. Nothing her father had said so far was the least bit helpful to Billy. In fact, it was as though he had dug the hole deeper.

"However," Zach said, "I've since changed my mind. I did enough checking to find out that my son-in-law is a hardworking, church-going man who spends most of his free time with his children. With three notable exceptions—all occurring since his wife's tragic death—he has been an outstanding citizen of this community.

"Although my son-in-law chose to start those three fights over the past year in bars, no one I talked to has ever seen him the least bit drunk. He has never hurt anyone seriously, and he has always paid for whatever damages there were. I know that doesn't excuse him entirely."

"Or at all," the judge interjected. "What I'd like to know is why Mr. Stonecreek started those fights."

"Only Billy himself knows the answer to that question. If I were guessing, I'd say he was a young man in a lot of pain and looking for a way to ease it."

"Then he chose the wrong way," the judge said. "All this is very interesting, but it doesn't explain why he was fighting within days of this hearing."

"To defend his wife's honor," Zach said.

Cherry's glance shot to Billy. He lowered his gaze to avoid hers, and a flush spread high on his cheekbones.

"I'm listening," the judge said.

"I was in Estes's Hardware Store yesterday when Billy came in. He picked up what he needed and went to the counter to pay. Ray Estes stood at the register and began making abusive, slanderous comments about my daughter, Cherry, in front of several other men, friends of Ray's, who were also waiting for service.

"Billy asked Ray to stop, but Ray continued provoking him, saying things to sully my daughter's reputation that no man could stand by and let another man say about his wife. Even then, Billy didn't throw the first punch.

"He told Ray he didn't want to fight, that he knew Ray was only mad because of what had happened the night Billy had kept him from assaulting Cherry. Billy said he would forget the insults if Ray would say he was sorry and hadn't meant what he'd said. Billy wanted the words taken back.

"Ray called Billy a coward, said he only fought men who were drunk. Even then, Your Honor, Billy kept his hands to himself. His fists were white-knuckled, but he didn't launch a blow.

"That's when Ray shoved him backward, and one of Ray's friends tripped him so he fell. Ray came over the counter and kicked him hard, while he was down. That was when Billy came up swinging. Ray's friends held his arms, so Ray could go at him. That's when he got the black eye.

"To tell you the truth, Your Honor, I took a few swings at those fellows myself. So you see, Billy tried to avoid a fight. He only got involved when it was a clear matter of self-defense."

Cherry gave her father a grateful look as he sat down, then met Billy's dark-eyed gaze. She reached for his hand under the table and clasped it tight. "Oh, Billy," she whispered. "Why didn't you tell me?"

"I shouldn't have let Ray provoke me," Billy muttered. "But I couldn't let him get away with saying those ugly things about you. I couldn't, Cherry."

She squeezed his hand. "It's all right, Billy. Surely the judge won't blame you now that he's heard the truth."

"I'll concede Mr. Stonecreek may have been provoked beyond endurance in this case," the judge said, confirming Cherry's hope. "The courts have conceded there are such things as 'fighting words' to which a man may respond justifiably with violence. And I'll take into consideration your suggestion that Mr. Stonecreek's other forays into fisticuffs may have been motivated by something other than drunkenness," the judge said.

"However," he continued, "I am concerned by several of Mrs. Trask's other accusations. Especially those concerning Mrs. Stonecreek's past behavior and her ability to function as a capable mother to two little girls."

"I'd like to speak on my wife's behalf, if I may," Billy said, rising to face the judge.

"Very well, Mr. Stonecreek," the judge replied.

"My daughters are lucky to have someone as wonderful as Cherry to be their mother," Billy said. "I feel myself fortunate to have her for my wife. Cherry was expelled from school for something she didn't do. Since then, she's taken care of Raejean and Annie during the day and gone to school every night to make up the classes she needs for graduation. I have every confidence that she'll complete her education with high marks and receive her diploma."

"I wasn't questioning your wife's intelligence," the judge said gently. "I'm more concerned about her maturity, her sense of responsibility, the example she'll set for the children."

Cherry saw Billy's Adam's apple bob as he swallowed hard. She wished she had led a different life. What could he say to defend her? She had been a troublemaker all her life. There was some truth in everything Mrs. Trask had said about her.

"I think Cherry's actions speak for themselves. My daughters are happy, healthy, and well-adjusted. Cherry treats them as though they were her own flesh and blood. You see, Your Honor, she knows what it feels like to lose your parents at a young age. She knows how important it is to make a child feel safe and secure and loved. That's what Cherry offers my children. Unconditional love. There's nothing more important to a child than knowing they're loved, is there, Your Honor?''

The judge cleared his throat. ''Yes, well, that's, true, of course.''

''But, Your Honor,'' Mrs. Trask protested, seeing the tide shifting. ''The same young woman whose merits Billy is extolling spent time in a juvenile detention facility. The fact remains, she was expelled from school. And she's only eighteen years old!''

''I will take all of that into consideration, Mrs. Trask,'' the judge promised. ''Does anyone have anything further to say? Very well. I will need some time in chambers to deliberate this matter. I'll have a decision for you shortly. Court is recessed.''

''All rise,'' the bailiff commanded.

Cherry rose on shaky legs and grabbed hold of Billy's hand for support. They had done all they could—which seemed precious little—to convince the judge they would be good parents. But was it enough?

One thing had become clear to Cherry. It wasn't only the children she was afraid to lose. She was afraid of losing Billy, too.

He had only married her temporarily to have a mother for his children. What role would there be for her in his life if his children were taken from him? Would she only be a painful reminder of what he had lost?

Cherry looked into Billy's eyes, all her fears naked for him to see. *Do you love me, Billy? If it weren't for the children, would you still want me for your wife?*

And found the reassurance she sought.

His love was visible in the reassuring warmth of his gaze, in the way he held firmly, supportively, to her hand, in the way he had defended her in court.

Without a word, Billy rose and pulled her into his embrace. His arms closed tight around her. "Don't leave me, Cherry," he whispered in her ear.

"I'm not going anywhere," she promised.

"I want us to be together forever."

"Forever? But—"

"No matter what happens here today, I want you with me. I love you, Cherry."

"I love you, too, Billy."

They held each other tight, offering strength and solace, parting only as the twins came hurtling down the aisle to greet them. Raejean leapt into Billy's arms, while Cherry scooped up Annie.

"Jewel says we have lots of aunts and uncles and cousins," Raejean announced. "Zillions of them!"

Cherry laughed. "Not quite that many."

"How many?" Annie asked.

"I don't know, exactly," Cherry said. "But lots."

"Can we go on a picnic now?" Raejean asked.

"Not yet," Billy said. "Soon."

"We have to go home first and change our clothes," Cherry reminded her.

"Can we leave now?" Annie asked. "Is the judge all done?"

"Almost," Cherry said. "He wants to think about things a little while before he makes up his mind."

"Makes up his mind about what?" Raejean asked.

Cherry and Billy exchanged a tormented glance.

Makes up his mind about whether to take you away from us.

Billy's heart had been thundering in his chest ever since the hearing began. He felt himself on the verge of panic, and the only thing he had to hang on to was Cherry's hand. So far, he had protected his daughters from knowing about the desperate courtroom struggle that would decide their future.

This morning, as he and Cherry had sipped coffee together at dawn, he had decided that even if the Trasks won custody, he would do his best to make the transition as amicable as possible. Surely the judge wouldn't deny him visitation rights, and he would continue to have a strong and loving relationship with his children.

Only, if there was one thing Billy had learned in this life, it was that there were no guarantees. He was terrified the judge would rule against him. He was terrified the Trasks would try to bar him from all contact with his children.

Right now he felt like taking Raejean and Annie and Cherry and running as far and as fast as he could. Fortunately, Cherry's family came to the rail that separated the spectators from the litigants, all of them talking at once, making escape impossible, even if he had succumbed to the urge.

He felt a hand on his shoulder and turned to find Zach Whitelaw standing behind him.

"I want to thank you for your words of support, sir," Billy said.

"It was my pleasure, son. I never had a chance to congratulate you on your wedding. I expect you to take good care of my daughter."

Billy would have answered if his jaw hadn't been clenched to keep his chin from quivering with emotion. Instead, he gave a jerky nod.

"The judge is coming back already, Dad," Colt said. "Wasn't it supposed to take longer?"

It had already been too long, as far as Billy was concerned, although he realized it had only been a matter of minutes since the judge had left the courtroom.

"We'd better get back to our seats," Zach said.

Billy was afraid to send his daughters away, afraid they weren't going to be his when he saw them again.

"All rise," the bailiff said.

Jewel was leading the children out of the courtroom when the judge said, "The children can stay."

Billy exchanged a quick look with Cherry and quickly gathered Raejean and Annie into the circle of his arms in front of him.

Cherry gave him a quavery smile. "Surely it's a good sign that the judge let them stay," she whispered as she slipped her arm around his waist. It was questionable who was supporting whom.

When the judge sat, Billy and Cherry sat, each of them holding one of the twins on their laps. They could hear the clock ticking as the judge shuffled papers.

Finally he looked up and said, "The circumstances of this case are unique. The grandparents of these children have a great deal to offer them, not the least of which is the experience to be gained with age. The children's father has shown a lack of judgment on occasion that makes his suitability as a parent questionable."

Billy's heart felt like it was going to pound right out of his chest. *He's going to give them to Penelope. I'm going to lose my children.*

"However," the judge continued, "the law favors the natural parents of a child over any other custodian. And there are other factors evident here that I believe have to be considered in my decision."

What is your decision, dammit? Billy raged inwardly.

"I've decided to leave custody of the minor children with their father," the judge announced.

Shouts of joy and clapping erupted behind Billy.

"I want quiet in the court," the judge said, pounding his gavel.

Billy was too stunned to move, his throat too tight to speak. He saw Cherry through a blurred haze of tears. She was laughing and crying at the same time.

"We won, Billy. We won!" Cherry sobbed.

"What did we win, Daddy?" Raejean said.

"Did we get a prize?" Annie asked.

"Quiet in the court," the judge repeated.

"Shh," Billy said to the girls. "Let's listen to the judge."

He was more than willing to listen, now that he knew his children were his to keep.

"There will be those who question my decision in light of the evidence heard here today about the actions of the children's father and stepmother. They have made mistakes in the past. However, they both seem dedicated to rectifying their behavior.

"So I have based my decision not on what either of them might have done in the past, but on what I saw here in this courtroom today that bodes well for the future.

"Seldom have I seen two individuals more supportive of each other, or more apparently devoted to each other. These children will have what too few children have these days—two parents who love and respect one another. I am convinced that these two young people are capable of providing a stable, healthy and happy home for the two minor children. Good luck to you both. Court is dismissed."

"All rise," the bailiff ordered.

Billy's knees were rubbery when he stood, and he slipped an arm around Cherry to keep himself upright. He realized he was grinning as he accepted the congratulatory slaps of the Whitelaws.

"Can we go on a picnic now?" Raejean asked.

"Soon," Cherry promised with a hiccuping laugh that was choked by tears of joy.

"Can Nana and Grampa Trask come, too?" Annie asked.

Billy looked across the room at the bitter face of Mrs. Trask and realized he only felt sorry for her. She had lost her daughter. Now she had lost her grandchildren, too. Because it would be a cold day in hell before he let her near his children again.

He felt Cherry's hand on his arm.

"The girls need their grandparents, Billy," she said. "And Mr. and Mrs. Trask need their grandchildren."

Billy struggled to be generous. He was still angry. And still afraid that the Trasks might yet find some way to take his children from him. But Cherry was right. Raejean and Annie loved their grandparents. It would be cruel to take them away. For their sakes, he had to forgive what the Trasks had tried to do.

"Why don't you go ask Nana and Grampa Trask if they'd like to come on our picnic with us?" Billy said to Raejean and Annie.

Billy pulled Cherry close against him as they watched the girls skip across the room to invite Penelope and Harvey Trask to join their picnic. Billy met Penelope's startled glance when she heard what the girls had to say. He saw her hesitate, then shake her head no and say something to the children.

Moments later the girls returned and Raejean said, "Nana says maybe next time."

Billy exchanged one last poignant look with Penelope before she turned away. Then he glanced down at Raejean and ruffled her hair. "Next time," Billy said.

Cherry met his eyes, her gaze proud and supportive, and said, "Next time for sure."

"Let's go home," Billy said as he reached for Cherry's hand. She reached out for Annie, and he reached out for Raejean. They walked out of the courtroom hand in hand in hand in hand, a family at last.

* * * * *

Dear Reader,

It has been so much fun over the past couple of years to create a multigenerational family, the Whitelaws of Hawk's Way, Texas, and share their trials and tribulations with you. I am especially pleased and proud to be a part of Desire's Celebration 1000, since I began writing for Desire almost ten years ago. My first Desire, *Fit To Be Tied,* was book #424. *The Temporary Groom* is #1004. We've all come a long way over the years, and it's been a glorious journey.

I'm a reader, as well as a writer, and I want to thank all those other Desire authors who have provided me with so much reading pleasure over the years. I feel very lucky to be one of you, and to have a chance to share my stories with others, as you have shared your stories with me.

Best wishes to Silhouette, a special thanks to my editor, Melissa Senate, to Lucia Macro, who heads the Desire line, and to all the hardworking editors, art directors, production assistants, salespeople and corporate leaders who have made Silhouette Desire novels such a pleasure to read and to write.

All my love,

Joan Johnston

COMING NEXT MONTH

#1009 THE COWBOY AND THE KID—Anne McAllister

July's *Man of the Month*, rodeo cowboy Taggart Jones, vowed never to remarry, but his little girl had other plans for him—and every one involved feisty schoolmarm Felicity Albright.

#1010 A GIFT FOR BABY—Raye Morgan

The Baby Shower

All Hailey Kingston wanted was to go to her friend's baby shower. Instead, she was stuck on a remote ranch, with a handsome cowboy as her keeper. But the longer she stayed in Mitch Harper's arms, the less she wanted to leave!

#1011 THE BABY NOTION—Dixie Browning

Daddy Knows Last

Priscilla Barrington wanted a baby, so she planned a visit to the town sperm bank. But then she met Jake Spencer! Could she convince the rugged cowboy to father her child—the old-fashioned way?

#1012 THE BRIDE WORE BLUE—Cindy Gerard

Northern Lights Brides

When Maggie Adams returned home, she never expected to see her childhood neighbor Blue Hazzard. Could the former gawky teenager turned hunk teach Maggie how to love again?

#1013 GAVIN'S CHILD—Caroline Cross

Bachelors and Babies

Gavin Cantrell was stunned to return home and learn that his estranged wife Annie had given birth to his child without telling him. Now that he was back, would his dream of being a family man be fulfilled?

#1014 MONTANA FEVER—Jackie Merritt

Made in Montana

Independent Lola Fanon never met anyone as infuriating—or as irresistible—as Duke Sheridan. She knew he wasn't her type, but staying away from the handsome rancher was becoming a losing battle....

Take 4 bestselling love stories FREE

Plus get a FREE surprise gift!

SILHOUETTE DESIRE® "CELEBRATION 1000" SWEEPSTAKES
OFFICIAL RULES—NO PURCHASE NECESSARY

To enter, complete an Official Entry Form or a 3"x5" card by hand printing "Silhouette Desire Celebration 1000 Sweepstakes," your name and address, and mail it to: In the U.S.: Silhouette Desire Celebration 1000 Sweepstakes, P.O. Box 9069, Buffalo, NY 14269-9069, or In Canada: Silhouette Desire Celebration 1000 Sweepstakes, P.O. Box 637, Fort Erie, Ontario L2A 5X3. Limit one entry per envelope. Entries must be sent via first-class mail and be received no later than 6/30/96. No liability is assumed for lost, late or misdirected mail.

Prizes: Grand Prize—an original painting (approximate value $1500 U.S.);300 Runner-up Prizes—an autographed Silhouette Desire® Book (approximate value $3.50 U.S./$3.99 CAN. each). Winners will be selected in a random drawing (to be conducted no later than 9/30/96) from among all eligible entries received by D.L. Blair, Inc., an independent judging organization whose decision is final.

Sweepstakes offer is open only to residents of the U.S. (except Puerto Rico) and Canada who are 18 years of age or older, except employees and immediate family members of Harlequin Enterprises Ltd., their affiliates, subsidiaries, and all agencies, entities and persons connected with the use, marketing or conduct of this sweepstakes. All federal, state, provincial, municipal and local laws apply. Offer void where prohibited by law. Taxes and/or duties are the sole responsibility of the winners. Any litigation within the province of Quebec respecting the conduct and awarding of prizes may be submitted to the Regie des alcools des courses et des jeux. All prizes will be awarded; winners will be notified by mail. No substitution for prizes is permitted. Odds of winning are dependent upon the number of eligible entries received.

Grand Prize winner must sign and return an Affidavit of Eligibility within 30 days of notification. In the event of noncompliance within this time period, prize may be awarded to an alternate winner. Any prize or prize notification returned as undeliverable may result in the awarding of that prize to an alternate winner. By acceptance of their prize, winners consent to the use of their names, photographs or likenesses for purposes of advertising, trade and promotion on behalf of Harlequin Enterprises Ltd., without further compensation unless prohibited by law. In order to win a prize, residents of Canada will be required to correctly answer a time-limited arithmetical skill-testing question administered by mail.

For a list of winners (available after October 31, 1996) send a separate self-addressed stamped envelope to: Silhouette Desire Celebration 1000 Sweepstakes Winners, P.O. Box 4200, Blair, NE 68009-4200.

SWEEPR

SILHOUETTE®

Desire®

CELEBRATION 1000

A treasured piece of romance could be yours!

During April, May and June as part of Desire's Celebration 1000 you can enter to win an original piece of art used on an actual Desire cover!

Or you could win one of 300 autographed Man of the Month books!

See Official Sweepstakes Rules for more details.

To enter, complete an Official Entry Form or a 3"x5" card by hand printing "Silhouette Desire Celebration 1000 Sweepstakes", your name and address, and mail to: **In the U.S.:** Silhouette Desire Celebration 1000 Sweepstakes, P.O. Box 9069, Buffalo, N.Y. 14269-9069, or **In Canada:** Silhouette Desire Celebration 1000 Sweepstakes, P.O. Box 637, Fort Erie, Ontario L2A 5X3. Limit one entry per envelope. Entries must be sent via first-class mail and be received no later than 6/30/96. No liability is assumed for lost, late or misdirected mail.

Official Entry Form—Silhouette Desire Celebration 1000 Sweepstakes

Name: _____

Address: _____

City: _____

State/Province: _____

Zip or Postal Code: _____

Favorite Desire Author: _____

Favorite Desire Book: _____

SWEEPS

SILHOUETTE... Where Passion Lives

Add these Silhouette favorites to your collection today!
Now you can receive a discount by ordering two or more titles!

SD#05819	WILD MIDNIGHT by Ann Major	$2.99	☐
SD#05878	THE UNFORGIVING BRIDE	$2.99 U.S.	☐
	by Joan Johnston	$3.50 CAN.	☐
IM#07568	MIRANDA'S VIKING by Maggie Shayne	$3.50	☐
SSE#09896	SWEETBRIAR SUMMIT	$3.50 U.S.	☐
	by Christine Rimmer	$3.99 CAN.	☐
SSE#09944	A ROSE AND A WEDDING VOW	$3.75 U.S.	☐
	by Andrea Edwards	$4.25 CAN.	☐
SR#19002	A FATHER'S PROMISE	$2.75	☐
	by Helen R. Myers		

(limited quantities available on certain titles)

TOTAL AMOUNT	$_____
DEDUCT: 10% DISCOUNT FOR 2+ BOOKS	$_____
POSTAGE & HANDLING	$_____
($1.00 for one book, 50¢ for each additional)	
APPLICABLE TAXES**	$_____
TOTAL PAYABLE	$_____
(check or money order—please do not send cash)	

To order, send the completed form with your name, address, zip or postal code, along with a check or money order for the total above, payable to Silhouette Books, to: **In the U.S.:** 3010 Walden Avenue, P.O. Box 9077, Buffalo, NY 14269-9077; **In Canada:** P.O. Box 636, Fort Erie, Ontario, L2A 5X3.

Name:_____

Address:_____City:_____

State/Prov.:_____ Zip/Postal Code:_____

**New York residents remit applicable sales taxes.
  Canadian residents remit applicable GST and provincial taxes.

Silhouette®
™

SBACK-JA2

You're About to Become a *Privileged Woman*

Reap the rewards of fabulous free gifts and benefits with proofs-of-purchase from Silhouette and Harlequin books

Pages & Privileges™

It's our way of thanking you for buying our books at your favorite retail stores.

PROOF OF PURCHASE

Offer expires October 31, 1996

SD-PP149

Harlequin and Silhouette—the most privileged readers in the world!

For more information about Harlequin and Silhouette's PAGES & PRIVILEGES program call the Pages & Privileges Benefits Desk: 1-503-794-2499

Silhouette®

SD-PP149